NEW TOEIC

新多益

閱讀測驗

大滿貫關鍵攻略：
擬真試題＋超詳解析

國家圖書館出版品預行編目資料

NEW TOEIC新多益閱讀測驗大滿貫關鍵攻略：
擬真試題+超詳解析 / 張文娟著. -- 初版.
-- 新北市 : 雅典文化, 民112.08
面 ； 公分. -- （英語工具書 ；20）
ISBN 978-626-7245-18-7 （平裝）

1. CTS: 多益測驗
805.1895   112008005

英語工具書系列 **20**

NEW TOEIC新多益閱讀測驗大滿貫關鍵攻略：擬真試題+超詳解析

著／張文娟
責任編輯／張文娟
內文排版／王國卿
封面設計／林鈺恆

法律顧問：方圓法律事務所／涂成樞律師

總經銷：永續圖書有限公司
永續圖書線上購物網
www.foreverbooks.com.tw

掃描填回函
好書隨時抽

出版日／2023年08月

雅典文化

22103　新北市汐止區大同路三段194號9樓之1
TEL　　（02）8647-3663
FAX　　（02）8647-3660

● 前言

　　多益的閱讀主要測驗於商業情境文件中快速尋找資訊的能力，因此，職場中常見的電子郵件、商業信件、新聞報導、廣告、公告、表格等等，都是常會出現的題型，最近更加入了線上對話紀錄，而且多篇閱讀的篇幅由兩篇增加至三篇，再再考驗閱讀速度與答題能力，也是對專注力的一大挑戰。本書將多益閱讀測驗部分 Part 5 & 6 與 Part 7 一一拆解，並且循序漸進傳授解題技巧，只要用心細細體會，就不會再出現沒有時間作答完的窘境；經過不斷演練，不但能於多益考試獲得亮眼的高分，真實工作時英文閱讀能力也會有同樣傑出的表現。

Chapter

6 破解閱讀 Part 7 各考題型式

Chapter 7 閱讀 Part 7 模擬試題 294

NEW TOEIC

Chapter **1**

NEW TOEIC 簡介

● 本章以 Q&A（問答方式）來解說新多益測驗：

Q 1 : 什麼是新多益英語測驗（TOEIC）？

A :

　　新多益英語測驗（TOEIC）全名為Test of English for International Communication，是美國教育測驗服務社（Educational Testing Service, ETS）針對母語非英語人士所研發的英語能力測驗，全球每年有超過700萬人次報考。

　　新多益系列測驗（The TOEIC Program）目前可於全球160個國家施測，至少為1萬4千個以上的企業客戶、教育單位及政府機構所採用。成績不僅具備信度與效度，也具有國際流通度，足以體現考生在實際溝通情境中的英語文能力。

　　TOEIC Listening and Reading Test本身並沒有所謂的「通過」或「不通過」，而是客觀地將受測者的能力以聽力5～495分、閱讀5～495分、總分10～990分的指標呈現，受測者也可以自評現在的英語能力，進而設定學習的目標分數。

Q 2 ： TOEIC 多益的測驗用途為何？

A ：

　　在真實的職場與校園環境中，當需要以英語溝通時，透過新多益系列測驗，成績使用單位能夠進一步掌握職員與學習者的能力現況。

　　也因為新多益系列測驗之國際流通度廣闊，眾多國內外企業、學校，皆採用新多益系列測驗作為評核人才英語程度之標準。

(一)求學加分條件

★ 升學加分證照

　　109 學年度大學個人申請簡章中，超過 1,000 個招生校系將「英文能力證明」列為審查資料或加分條件，善用新多益系列測驗成績，點亮大學甄選、四技二專甄選備審資料。

★ 登錄學習歷程

　　自 108 學年度起，教育部高中生學習歷程資料庫正式全面上線，新多益系列測驗成績可登錄「高中數位學習歷程檔案資料庫」，作為學生的多元表現認證之一，且登錄數量無上限。

★ 大學英文免修門檻、英語班級程度分班

國內超過百所大學採用新多益系列測驗作為英文課程免修門檻；學校亦可用新多益系列測驗成績作為大一英語分班標準。

(二)求職加分條件

★ 求職履歷加分，提升職場競爭力

據調查，400家年營收超過1億元新台幣的企業中，超過六成（62.1%）企業招募新人會參考英語成績。且要求新進員工平均新多益成績為 582 分。想展現求職優勢者，可運用新多益成績點亮履歷，在眾多競爭者中脫穎而出。

★ 就業升遷標準、企業人才管理工具

2012至2018年，使用新多益系列測驗的企業逐漸增加，2018 年有 36%的企業選擇新多益系列測驗掌握員工實際的英語程度，作為企業員工招募、升遷及外派標準、企業人才管理工具。

★ 教學管理、人才篩選標準

★ 英語文教學管理指標

英語教學機構可善用新多益系列測驗落實英語能力管理，作為英語課程前測、教學成果評量，以及英語培訓績效檢驗標準。

★ 國際志工選拔評量標準

舉凡國際會議、體育賽事等活動，採用新多益系列測驗成績作為選拔國際志工的標準。運用新多益成績突顯英語優勢，爭取參與國際活動的機會。

Q 3 : TOEIC 多益的研發製作單位為何？

ETS®是目前全球規模最大的一所非營利教育測驗及評量單位，在全球180多個國家／地區提供服務，每年開發、管理和評分超過5000萬次考試。

ETS®專精教學評量及測驗心理學、教育政策之研究，在教學研究領域上居於領導地位，擁有教育專家、語言學家、統計學家、心理學家等成員約3,200名。其研發的測驗及語言學習產品包括：TOEFL iBT® Test、TOEFL ITP® Tests、TOEFL Junior® Standard Tests、TOEFL® Primary™ Tests、TOEIC® Tests、TOEIC Bridge® Tests、SAT®、GRE® 測驗等，以及CRITERION®。

Q 4 : TOEIC 多益的測驗內容為何？

A :

本測驗針對母語非英語人士所設計，測驗題型反映全球現有日常生活中，社交及職場之英語使用情況。測驗題型多元化，涵蓋多種場合、地點與狀況。能檢驗出考生目前或未來在真實情境中所需的國際溝通力。

TOEIC® Listening and Reading Test 共 200 題，皆為單選題，分為聽力及閱讀兩大部分，測驗時間約 2 小時 30 分鐘（含基本資料及問卷填寫）。

TOEIC Listening and Reading Test			
《聽力測驗》	**Part1** 照片描述	**Part2** 應答問題	**Part3** 簡短對話	**Part4** 簡短獨白
《閱讀測驗》	**Part5** 句子填空	**Part6** 段落填空	**Part7** 閱讀測驗	

聽力測驗

包含 4 大題，共 100 個單選題，測驗時間約為 45 分鐘，內容包含四種口音，以及多種題型如應答問題、簡短對話等。

大題	題型	題數
1	照片描述	6 題
2	應答問題	25 題
3	簡短對話	39 題(3x13)
4	簡短獨白	30 題(3x10)

閱讀測驗

包含 3 大題，共 100 個單選題，測驗時間為 75 分鐘。內容包含網頁、通訊軟體、網站等閱讀題材，並依個人能力調配閱讀及答題速度。

大題	題型	題數
5	句子填空	30 題
6	段落填空	16 題(4x4)
7	單篇閱讀	29 題
	多篇閱讀	25 題

Q 5：TOEIC 多益的測驗情境有哪些？

A：

企業發展	研究、產品研發
外食	商務／非正式午餐、宴會、招待會、餐廳訂位
娛樂	電影、劇場、音樂、藝術、展覽、博物館、媒體
金融／預算	銀行業務、投資、稅務、會計、帳單
一般商務	契約、談判、併購、行銷、銷售、保證、商業企劃、會議、勞動關係
保健	醫療保險、看醫生、牙醫、診所、醫院
房屋／公司地產	建築、規格、購買租賃、電力瓦斯服務
製造業	工廠管理、生產線、品管
辦公室	董事會、委員會、信件、備忘錄、電話、傳真、電子郵件、辦公室器材與家俱、公室流程
人事	招考、雇用、退休、薪資、升遷、應徵與廣告、津貼、獎勵
採購	購物、訂購物資、送貨、發票
技術層面	電子、科技、電腦、實驗室與相關器材、技術規格
旅遊	火車、飛機、計程車、巴士、船隻、渡輪、票務、時刻表、車站、機場廣播、租車、飯店、預定、脫班與取消

Q 6 : TOEIC 多益的測驗如何計分？

A :

　　考生用鉛筆在答案卡上作答。測驗分數取決於由答對題數決定，再將每一大類（聽力類、閱讀類）答對題數轉換成分數，範圍在5到495分之間。兩大類加起來即為總分，範圍在10到990分之間，答錯不倒扣。

證書說明

　　TOEIC證書中列出聽力與閱讀的分項分數及總分，依考生成績分為五種顏色，是職場競爭力的最佳證明，測驗日起兩年內都可申請。

證書分類

- 金色 860～990分
- 藍色 730～855分
- 綠色 470～725分
- 棕色 220～465分
- 橘色 10～215分

Q 7 : TOEIC 多益成績如何反映英語能力？

A :

多益成績與英語能力對照表

TOEIC® 成績	語言能力	證照顏色
905~990	英語能力十分近似於英語母語人士，能夠流暢有條理表達意見、參與談話，主持英文會議、調和衝突並做出結論，語言使用上即使有瑕疵，亦不會造成理解上的困擾。	金色(860~990)
785~900	可有效地運用英文滿足社交及工作上所需，措辭相當、表達流暢；但在某些情形下，如：面臨緊張壓力、討論話題過於冷僻艱澀時，仍會顯現出語言能力不足的情況。	金色(860~990) 藍色(730~855)
605~780	可以英語進行一般社交場會的談話，能夠應付例行性的業務需求、參加英文會議、聽取大部分要點；但無法流利的以英語發表意見、作辯論，使用的詞彙、句型也以一般常見為主。	藍色(730~855) 綠色(470~725)
405~600	英文文字溝通能力尚可，會話方面稍嫌詞彙不足、語句簡單，但已能掌握少量相關語言，可以從事英語相關程度較低的工作。	綠色(470~725) 棕色(220~465)
255~400	語言能力僅僅侷限在簡單的一般日常生活對話，同時無法做連續性交談，亦無法用英文工作。	棕色(220~465) 橘色(10~215)
10~250	只能以背誦的句子進行問答而不能自行造句，尚無法將英文當作溝通工具來使用。	橘色(10~215)

Q 8 : 台灣各行各業對多益分數的要求為何？

A :

（一） TOEIC 多益測驗約 100-215 分＝初級

　　有基礎英語能力，能理解和使用淺易日常用語，英語能力相當於國中畢業者。一般行政助理、維修技術人員、百貨業、餐飲業、旅館業或觀光景點服務人員、計程車駕駛等。

（二） TOEIC 多益測驗約 220-465 分＝中級

　　具有使用簡單英語進行日常生活溝通的能力，英語能力相當於高中職畢業者。一般地勤行政、業務、技術、銷售人員、護理人員、旅館、飯店接待人員、總機人員、警政人員、旅遊從業人員等。

（三） TOEIC 多益測驗約 470-725 分＝中高級

　　英語能力相當於大學非英語主修系所畢業者。商務、企劃人員、祕書、工程師、研究助理、空服人員、航空機師、航管人員、海關人員、導遊、外事警政人員、新聞從業人員、資訊管理人員等。

(四) TOEIC 多益測驗約 730-855 分＝高級

英語能力相當於國內大學英語主修系所或曾赴英語系國家大學或研究所進修並取得學位者。高級商務人員、協商談判人員、英語教學人員、研究人員、翻譯人員、外交人員、國際新聞從業人員等。

(五) TOEIC 多益測驗約 860-990 分＝優級

英語能力接近受過高等教育之母語人士，各種場合均能使用適當策略作最有效的溝通。專業翻譯人員、國際新聞特派人員、外交官員、協商談判主談人員等。

以上資料來源為http://www.toeic.com.tw/

NEW TOEIC

Chapter 2

新制 NEW TOEIC

● 本章以 Q&A（問答方式）來解說改版後的新多益：

Q 1 ： 2018 年 3 月為什麼會推出改版的新多益？

A ：

　　為確保測驗符合考生及成績使用單位之需求，ETS定期重新檢視所有試題內容。TOEIC®Listening and Reading Test題型更新，反映了全球現有日常生活中社交及職場之英語使用情況。作為一個評量日常生活或職場情境之英語測驗，依然維持相同的公平性、效度以及信度。本次測驗更新，題型雖有所改變，但測驗的難易度、測驗時間或測驗分數所代表的意義將不會有所變動。

　　由於英語的使用及溝通方法不斷改變，為了確保TO-EIC® Listening and Reading Test能夠反映出時下英語使用的狀況，ETS®更新了部分題型，與時俱進地加入過去十年間經常使用的溝通用語，包括文字簡訊、即時通訊及多人對話等等。 台灣地區自2018年3月份公開測驗開始實施。

Q 2 ： 2018 改版後的新多益測驗題型變更為何？

A ：

　　2018 新制新多益考題數量 200題&考試時間不變 120分鐘。

題型 5 大改變：

1. 聽力照片＆應答題大幅減少
2. 聽力對話從 2 人，增加為 3 人對話
3. 聽力對話 & 獨白加入圖表
4. 閱讀的短文填空仿照托福，加入全新句子插入題
5. 閱讀測驗新增多篇閱讀（3 篇以上文章）

《重點整理》2018 新新多益題型變更

	題型	改制前	2018 改制後 題數	差別
聽力測驗：45分鐘				
Part 1	照片題	10題	6題	題數減少
Part 2	應答題	30題	25題	題數減少
Part 3	短對話	3題 (共10組)	3題 (共13組)	題數增加 加入 3 人對話 加入圖表
Part 4	短獨白	3題 (共10組)	3題 (共10組)	加入圖表
閱讀測驗：75分鐘				
Part 5	單句填空	40題	30題	題數大幅減少
Part 6	短文填空	12題 (共3篇)	16題 (共4篇)	題數增加 新增「插入句子題」
Part 7	閱讀測驗	單篇閱讀 共28題	單篇閱讀 共29題	題數增加
		雙篇閱讀 共20題	多篇閱讀 共25題	題數增加 增加多篇閱讀

Q 3 ： 2018 改版後的新多益測驗是不是變得比較難？

A ：

　　2018 新制新多益測驗除了部分題型減少題數，聽力 & 閱讀的部分也分別融入新題型，但考試時間不變，所以難度會提升很多。

　　以往比較好拿分的題型大幅減少題數，出題方式更靈活、貼近生活，考試需要有良好的英文聽力、閱讀，以及聽讀的整合能力，所以你不但要提升自己的英文能力，閱讀、思考的速度，還有答題速度也要加快很多。新多益成績雖然沒有有效時限，但是現在企業和學校大多要求兩年內的新多益證書，有的甚至更要求要一年內的，關於有效時間的問題，請先詢問一下你的公司或學校。

Q 4 ： 2018 改版後的新多益測驗閱讀考題哪裡改變？

A ：

1. Part 5 題數大幅減少
2. Part 6 題數增加；新增「插入句子題」
3. Part 7 閱讀測驗
   單篇：題數增加；增加線上聊天或即時訊息；新增「插入句子題」。
   雙篇：題數增加；增加多篇閱讀；新增「插入句子題」。

Q 5： 2018 改版後的新新多益測驗閱讀考題如何準備？

A：

1. 平時要保持對職場可接觸到的英文有種高度敏感，例如商業電子郵件、公告、廣告等等，還有養成閱讀英文報紙的好習慣，至少瀏覽標題和結論，訓練閱讀速度，快速抓出重點，隨學隨記。

2. 多加留意社群媒體常用的英語用法，如果有使用通訊軟體或視訊開會，請多留意線上英語交談用法。

以上資料來源為http://www.toeic.com.tw/

NEW TOEIC

Chapter ③

閱讀英文的要點

●一、掌握文法

　　要理解英文詞句,首先要找出句子的主詞與動詞,通常主詞不會太難找,但是主要動詞則不一定很明顯,但是如果配合一些文法知識與拆解句子技巧,仍然可以很輕易將動詞找出來。例如:

　　★有時態變化的就是主要動詞。

　　★助動詞後經常接主要動詞。

　　★現在分詞與過去分詞子句帶出的主要動詞。

　　★拆解有連接詞的句子或多個子句的句子,以得到主要動詞。

●二、速讀技巧

　　速讀需要瀏覽技巧,依照所搜尋內容不同分為略讀和掃讀:

　　略讀(skimming):搜尋較為籠統的大意,例如題目問說這封電子郵件的目的是什麼,或是這篇報導的主旨為何。

　　掃讀(scanning):搜尋特定的細節資訊,例如題目問說希望收信者最晚什麼時候回覆,時間、地點經常是掃讀要找的目標。

　　閱讀測驗的問題與選項通常不會用一模一樣的單字或片語，而是會以同義字或「換句話說」（Paraphrasing）的方式來表達。

●三、專注力

1. 積極態度與動機

　　就像學習任何學科與技能，抱有積極正向態度較容易成功，被動的人則較容易遇到困難就中途而廢。有動機後要設立可行的目標，包含短程與長程目標，有了目標才可以隨時修正方法與路線。

2. 注意力

　　將外在環境整理好，有助於集中注意力學習；將內在心境調整好，有助於聚焦於所要學習的材料上。內外條件皆具備，學習也就能上軌道了。

3. 重複

　　重複練習在語言學習上非常重要，就像學任何一樣樂器，只要有恆心勤加練習，無論天生音感如何，終究是學得會的。

4. 鬆緊適中

　　學習的時候不要太緊張或太放鬆，就像樂器上的弦要鬆緊適中，才能發揮最好功效。

四、學習方式

1. 以速讀方式來閱讀，不應該會影響理解文章的能力。

2. 每個型式的文章都有特定的起承轉合，除非是多篇且總篇幅過長，否則都建議先讀測驗題目和選項，如果沒有時間至少要先讀測驗題目，然後以略讀和掃讀快速瀏覽文章，就能很快找到答案。

3. 瀏覽文章時，養成先看標題和標題下的敘述，第一段和最後一段的開始與結束，以及每段的開端，這樣非常有助於快速理解整篇文章大意。

4. 字彙與文法

   平時可以充實字根字首知識。

   針對多益整理的字彙來學習，最好按主題分類，例如出差和辦公室等等。

   文法對高中畢業後很久沒有接觸英文的人來說，不是個容易的項目，建議複習一下基本文法，重溫高中文法即可。

5. 檢討錯過的題目

   平時做的考古題，不要做完就算了，最好常常回去檢討做錯過的題目，才不會重蹈覆轍。

6. 文章的起承轉合

不需要背文章，但是要多多重複閱讀，久了自然熟悉商用文章，例如廣告和電子郵件等等，植入文章語感於腦海。

● 五、記憶

1. 聯想記憶法

將新訊息連結至已知訊息，例如字首字根的字彙學習。

2. 重複記憶法

請找出最適合自己學習與記憶的時間，一般會推薦在睡前來進行記憶，第二天一早起來則複習，行有餘力按順序複習前幾天記憶的內容。

NEW TOEIC

Chapter 4

Part 5 單句填空 &
Part 6 短文填空

●Part 5 單句填空

重點提示：

　　Part 5 單句填空大致可分為測驗單字詞性和單字意思兩種類型。

　　◎如果是測驗單字詞性，由答案選項馬上可以看出來，例如：

1. She was _____ in the rain on her way to the office.

(A) catches　　　　(B) catch

(C) catching　　　(D) caught

詳解

　　答案選項都是同一個單字的變化形，代表要測驗的是單字時態，意思是被雨淋到：be caught in the rain，正確答案為 (D) caught。

翻譯

她在進辦公室途中被雨淋到了。

(D)　遭遇到

2. He might come across as a rude customer, but his requests seem to be rather _____ to me.

(A) reason　　　　(B) reasonable

(C) reasonably　　(D) unreasonable

詳解

　　在be動詞後面應該要接的是形容詞，(A) reason是名詞：理由，也是動詞：思考；在所有選項中只有 (B) reasonable與 (D) unreasonable為形容詞，而根據句意，答案應該是(B)合理的；(C)以 "ly" 結尾，明顯是副詞：合理地。

解釋

　　他可能有點像是個無理的顧客，但是他的要求對我來說似乎相當合理。

　　(B) 合理的

3. Quite a few people are _____ about the rapid advancement of AI, short for Artificial Intelligence.

　　(A) concerns
　　(B) concerned
　　(C) concerning
　　(D) concern

詳解

　　在這裡要測驗的是be concerned about這個形容詞片語，意思是為某事感到憂心，concern可以當憂慮的名詞與動詞（憂慮某事），而concerning 則是concern的現在分詞，在這裡都不適用。

翻譯

　　不少人對於AI的快速進展感到憂心，AI就是人工智慧。

　　(B) 憂心的

◎如果是測驗單字意思，也可由答案選項馬上可以看出來，例如：

I wish I could explain this issue in a less _____ way.

(A) complicated   (B) easy

(C) causal   (D) comfortable

選項都是形容詞，都符合空格處需要的詞性，由此可知，此處要測驗的是單字的意思，(A) complicated 複雜的；(B) easy 容易的；(C) casual 輕鬆的；(D) comfortable舒適的，正確答案為 (A)。整句的意思是：要是我可以不用那麼複雜的方式來解釋這議題就好了。

綜合以上可以得知，不論是哪類題型，先讀答案選項再讀題目，通常能較有效率來作答。

●文法整理

以下的文法整理在單句填空上很基礎也很重要：

Unit 1   名詞
Unit 2   代名詞
Unit 3   動詞
Unit 4   形容詞

Unit 1 名詞

● 一、名詞的定義

　　表示人、事、物、地點、抽象概念等名稱的詞，稱為名詞。

● 二、名詞的種類

　　名詞可以分為專有名詞和普通名詞：

　　名詞主要分為兩大類：專有名詞和普通名詞。專有名詞是指「特定」的名稱，第一個字母通常必須大寫；普通名詞則是指「一般」的名稱，第一個字母通常不須大寫，除非是在句子的開頭或是作為標題時。

1. 專有名詞 (Proper Nouns)

代表獨一無二的名稱，第一個字母要大寫，例如：Jessica 潔西卡（女性名字），Friday 星期五，Thanksgiving 感恩節，Christmas 聖誕節，Taipei 台北，Tokyo 東京⋯⋯

2. 普通名詞 (Common Nouns)

A. 具體名詞 (Concrete Nouns)

代表某類具體人、事、物中的個體，例如：pencil 鉛筆，girl 女孩， school 學校，hospital 醫院⋯⋯

B. 集合名詞 (Collective Nouns)

代表許多個體組合成的集合體，例如：family 家庭，class 班級，staff 全體員工，committee 委員會⋯⋯

C. 抽象名詞 (Abstract Nouns)

代表之物無具體形狀，常為一抽象概念，例如：love 愛，hate 恨，peace 和平⋯⋯

D. 物質名詞 (Material Nouns)

代表由某材料所組成，無法用單位數量詞計數的物質，例如：water 水，milk 牛奶，coffee 咖啡，gold 金，silver 銀⋯⋯

專有名詞和普通名詞對照表	
普通名詞	專有名詞
city (城市)	**Taipei** (台北)
car (車子)	**Ford** (福特)
company (公司)	**Facebook** (臉書)
weekday (工作日)	**Tuesday** (星期二)
uncle (舅舅、叔叔)	**Uncle Tom** (湯姆叔叔)
river (河流)	**Tamsui River** (淡水河)
temple (寺廟)	**Longshan Temple** (龍山寺)
tablet (平板電腦)	**iPad** (蘋果公司產品)

● 三、可數名詞與不可數名詞

1. 可數名詞 (Countable Nouns)

　　大部分名詞都是可數名詞，意即這些名詞所代表之人、事、物可以計數。單數名詞之前要加冠詞：a（名詞字首為子音）, an（名詞字首為母音）；複數名詞之後要變為複數形式。

2. 不可數名詞 (Uncountable Nouns)

　　無法計數，單數名詞之前不可加冠詞（a, an）；複數名詞之後不可變為複數形式。抽象與物質名詞皆屬於不可數名詞。

3. 可作可數也可作不可數名詞

A. 有些名詞可作可數也可作不可數名詞，但意思不同。

例如：coffee 咖啡

I like to drink coffee in the morning.（表示一般的咖啡，不可數）

I'd like to have 2 coffees.（表示兩杯咖啡）

B. 有些名詞表示整體物質時，是不可數名詞；表示某物質的一例時是可數名詞。

例如：hair 頭髮

He has black hair.（指的是整頭黑色的頭髮）

He found a hair in the hamburger.（指的是單根的頭髮）

He has quite a few white hairs.（指的是一根根的頭髮）

四、名詞的單複數形式

1. 通常於名詞字尾加 s。例如：pen, pens 筆；student, students 學生；town, towns 鎮……

2. 名詞若以 s, sh〔ʃ〕, ch〔tʃ〕, x, z 結尾，則於名詞字尾加 es。例如：dish, dishes 餐點；church,

churches 教堂；box, boxes 盒子……

◎但是如果字尾 ch 發音為〔k〕，則於名詞字尾加 s。例如：stomach, stomachs 胃; monarch, monarchs 君主……

3. 名詞若以子音加上 o 結尾，則於名詞字尾加 es。例如：tomato, tomatoes 番茄；potato, potatoes 馬鈴薯；hero, heroes 英雄……

◎但是如果字尾為母音加上 o 結尾，則於名詞字尾加 s。例如：radio, radios 收音機；studio, studios 工作室；zoo, zoos 動物園……

4. 名詞若以子音加上 y 結尾，則將 y 改為 i，再加 es。例如：story, stories 故事； dragonfly, dragonflies 蜻蜓； family, families 家庭……

◎但是名詞若以母音加上 y 結尾，只加 s。例如：boy, boys 男孩；day, days 日子；ray, rays 光線……

5. 名詞若以 f, fe 結尾，則將 f, fe 改為 v，再加 es。例如：half, halves 半個；knife, knives 刀；life, lives 生命……

6. 通常以複數形式出現的名詞，例如：pants 褲子；glasses 眼鏡；scissors 剪刀……

7. 有些名詞以 -ics 結尾，但是卻並非複數，例如：athletics, economics, electronics, gymnastics, mathematics, physics, politics。

8. 有些名詞以 -s 結尾，但是可以視情形與單數或複數動詞連用，例如：means, series, species。

9. 有些單數名詞經常會接複數動詞，例如：audience, committee, company, family, firm, government, staff, team。

10. 單複數形式相同的名詞

例如：

one sheep - two sheep　綿羊

one deer - two deer　鹿

one fish - two fish　魚

one cattle - two cattle　牛

one trout - two trout　鱒魚

one Chinese - two Chinese　中國人

one corps - two corps　軍團

one species - two species　物種

11. 複數變化不規則名詞

★ 改變母音

man - men 男人；woman - women 女人；
goose - geese 鵝；foot - feet 腳；
mouse - mice 老鼠；louse - lice 蝨子……

★ 字尾加 -en或 -ren

ox - oxen 牛；child - children 小孩

★ 字尾為 -sis 改為 -ses

crisis - crises 危機；oasis - oases 綠洲； analysis - analyses 分析；thesis - theses 論文；basis - bases 基礎；hypothesis - hypotheses 假設

★ 字尾為 -us 改為 -i

alumnus - alumni 校友；syllabus - syllabi 課程表；stimulus - stimuli 刺激；radius - radii 半徑；fungus - fungi 真菌

★ 字尾為 -um 改為 -a

datum - data 數據；medium - media 媒體；curriculum - curricula 課程；bacteria - bacterium 細菌；memorandum - memoranda 備忘錄

★ 字尾為 -on 改為 -a

phenomenon - phenomena 現象；criterion - criteria 標準

★ 字尾為 -a 改為 -ae

alumna - alumnae 女校友；formula - formulae 公式

★ 字尾為 -e 改為 -ce

die - dice 骰子

★ 字尾為 -x 改為 -ces

appendix - appendices/appendixes 附錄；

index - indices/indexes 索引

1. The police _____ soon called by a passerby after the robber mugged the old woman.

(A) is   (B) are

(C) were   (D) was

詳解

在此處的the police 屬於集合名詞，代表the police people 所以要用複數動詞，因為句意是過去時態，所以要用過去式。

翻譯

搶匪搶了老婦人後，路人馬上叫了警察。

(C) be動詞的過去複數

2. Mathematics _____ her such a big headache when she was in high school.

(A) give   (B) gives

(C) given   (D) gave

詳解

Mathematics數學（學科名）雖然以s結尾，但是屬於單數名詞，要用單數動詞，句意為過去在高中時，所以要用過去式。

翻譯

高中時數學曾經讓她頭痛不已。

(D) 給（過去式）

3. **In this university most students are used to ____ ____ part-time to support themselves.**

(A) work (B) working

(C) works (D) worked

詳解

此處要測驗的是 be used to（習慣於）片語後要加動名詞，所以答案為 (B) working。

翻譯

在這所大學大部分學生都習慣打工來賺生活費。

(B) 工作

4. **The woman took her doctor's _____ to bring her husband along for the next consultation.**

(A) advising (B) advices

(C) advise (D) advice

詳解

建議的動詞為 advise，名詞為 advice，是不可數名詞，如果要說一個建議，要說 a piece of advice。

翻譯

　　這個婦人接受醫師的建議，下次帶她先生一起去諮商。

　　(D) 建議

5. She likes this pair of _____ with many holes.

　　(A) jean 　　　　　　(B) a jean

　　(C) jeans 　　　　　　(D) the jean

詳解

　　一條牛仔褲的英文要說a pair of jeans，因為褲子有兩條褲管，所以要用複數。

翻譯

　　她喜歡這件有很多洞的牛仔褲。

　　(C) 牛仔褲

6. The new director's _____ are often described by journalists as "out of fashion".

　　(A) clothes 　　　　　(B) cloth

　　(C) cloths 　　　　　(D) clothe

詳解

　　英文的clothes（衣服）要用複數動詞，而clothing表示某種衣服，則要用單數動詞。

翻譯

新主任的衣服常被記者形容是「跟不上流行」。

(A) 衣服

7. Currently the teaching staff of this private school _____ from all over the world.

(A) is　　　　　　　(B) are

(C) was　　　　　　(D) were

詳解

這裡的staff屬於集合名詞，表示所有的教職人員，所以要用be動詞複數現在式are。

翻譯

目前這所小學的教職人員來自全世界。

(B) 教職人員

8. The boss seems to be pleased with one of our _____ of the financial market, so we do not have to do it again.

(A) analysis　　　　(B) analyses

(C) analyze　　　　(D) analyzes

詳解

介系詞後要接名詞，因為是在one of（其中之一）之後，所以要接analysis（分析）的複數形analyses；analyze

則為動詞，analyzes則為第三人稱單數的動詞形式。

翻譯

　　老闆似乎對我們財金市場分析其中之一感到滿意，所以我們不必再做一次。

　　(B) 分析

---

9. **Once you arrive in the country, make sure you open a _____ account.**

　　(A) savings　　　　(B) saving

　　(C) savers　　　　(D) saver

詳解

　　儲蓄帳號的英文是savings account，這是固定用法。

翻譯

　　你一到達這國家，一定要去開一個儲蓄帳戶。

　　(A) 儲蓄

---

10. **In the beginning, this student made quite a few _____ in Grammar, but soon she made huge improvement.**

　　(A) mistake　　　　(B) mistook

　　(C) mistaking　　　(D) mistakes

詳解

在quite a few（不少的）之後要用複數可數名詞，表示為數可觀的某種可數名詞，在這裡是mistake（錯誤）的複數形mistakes。

翻譯

剛開始時，這個學生在文法上犯了不少錯誤，但不久後她就進步良多。

(D) 錯誤

Unit 2 代名詞

代名詞的分類如下：

一、人稱代名詞
二、指示代名詞
三、反身代名詞

人稱代名詞變化詳細表格如下：

人稱 性、 數、格	主格	所有格	受格	所有代名詞	反身格	中文
第一(單)	I	my	me	mine	myself	我
第一(複)	we	our	us	ours	ourselves	我們
第二(單)	you	your	you	yours	yourself	你
第二(複)	you	your	you	yours	yourselves	你們
第三(男單)	he	his	him	his	himself	他
第三(女單)	she	her	her	hers	herself	她
第三(中單)	one	one's	one	...	oneself	一個人；任何人
第三(男/女單)	he she	his her	him her	his hers	himself herself	他或她
第三(中單)	it	its	it	its	itself	它；牠
第三(複)	they	their	them	theirs	themselves	他們

一、人稱代名詞

人稱代名詞顧名思義是主要用來代替人稱的代替名詞，也可以用來代替物：

I, me

you, you

he, him,

she, her

It

we, us

they them

例句：

例 Gray had a serious cold, and Gray had to take a day off.

蓋瑞重感冒，蓋瑞必須請假一天。

替代後-->

Gray had a serious cold, and he had to take a day off.

蓋瑞重感冒，他必須請假一天。

人稱代名詞可以用來代替物或動物，例如she, her, he, him, it, they, them。

例 She is a fancy yacht, isn't it?
她是艘豪華的遊艇，對吧？

例 They are the missing children.
他們就是失蹤的孩子。

此外 one, ones 可以作代名詞，代替上下文中的名詞，還可作不定代名詞表示任何人。

例 There came several students. Do you know the one with a basketball hat?
那邊有幾個學生走過來，你認識那個戴著棒球帽的那個學生嗎？

例 One should never underestimate the importance of health.
我們不該輕估健康的重要性。

比較特別的是所有格代名詞：

mine ＝ my ＋ 名詞

yours ＝ your ＋ 名詞

his ＝ his ＋ 名詞

hers ＝ her ＋ 名詞

his or hers ＝ his or her ＋ 名詞

its ＝ its ＋ 名詞

ours ＝ our ＋ 名詞

theirs ＝ their ＋ 名詞

例句：

例 This cup is hers. Yours is on that table.

= This is her cup. Your cup is on that table.
這杯子是她的；你的在那張桌子上。

例 Those books are theirs. Ours are over there.

= Those are their books. Our books are over there.
那些書是他們的；我們的在那邊。

● 二、指示代名詞

指示代名詞 this、that、these、those

這些字用來當作指示代名詞時，this、that用來當作單數指示代名詞，而these、those用來當作複數指示代名詞。其中this、these代表靠近我們這裡的人或東西，that、those代表離我們較遠的人或東西。

	單數	複數
近	**this**	**these**
遠	**that**	**Those**

例句：

例 These items are more expensive than those.
這些物品比那些貴。

其中this、that 也可以代表以上所述的陳述，例如：

　　Recently AI has been applied in many fields, and this is especially obvious in household supplies.

　　He got a serious cold, and because of that, he could not attend this meeting.

　　如果要作為比較的單數代名詞要用that；如果要作為比較的複數代名詞則要用those。

例句：

例 The population of Tokyo is more than that of Taipei.
東京的人口比台北的多。

例 The books of the library are older than those of the bookstore.
這間圖書館的書比那間書店的還要舊。

●三、反身代名詞

反身代名詞有以下幾種：

單數	複數
myself	**ourselves**
yourself	**yourselves**
herself, himself, itself, oneself	**themselves**

例句：

例 I cut myself in the kitchen.
　我在廚房割到手。

例 You don't have to do everything yourself.
　你不需要每件事都親自做。

例 The work itself is not hard, but it is hard for the team members to do it together.
　這工作本身不難，但是要叫團隊成員合作卻很難。

1. Most jewelry in this store is unaffordable to me, but I like to admire _____ in window shopping.

(A) it　　　　　　(B) them

(C) itself　　　　(D) themselves

翻譯

　　這家店的大部分珠寶我都買不起，但是我喜歡只瀏覽商店櫥窗而不買。

(A) 它

2. The employer with a staff of more than 4 people should provide _____ with labor and health insurance.

(A) It　　　　　　(B) they

(C) them　　　　(D) him

翻譯

　　超過四個員工的雇主必須要提供員工勞保和健保。

(C) 他們

3. Make sure you check _____ belongings before leaving the library.

(A) yourself　　　(B) your

(C) yours　　　　(D) yourselves

翻譯

離開圖書館前一定要檢查您的所有物。

(B) 你的

4. I think Jack is the right person for the job because of _____ credentials.

    (A) their   (B) himself

    (C) him   (D) his

翻譯

我認為傑克是這工作的最佳人選，因為他的學經歷。

(D) 他的

5. On the class reunion, almost all people brought _____ spouses with them.

    (A) theirs   (B) their

    (C) them   (D) themselves

翻譯

幾乎所有的人都帶了他們的伴侶來參加同學會。

(B) 他們的

6. Jenny always designs Christmas cards by _____.

    (A) her   (B) herself

    (C) hers   (D) she

翻譯

珍妮總是自己設計聖誕卡。

(B)

7. The janitor found _____ locked in the room and he did not have the key to the door.

(A) him   (B) himself

(C) his   (D) he

翻譯

這個工友發現他被鎖在房間內,而他沒帶房間的鑰匙。

(B) 他自己

8. In the ceremony, the CEO awarded the distinguished staff members _____.

(A) themselves   (B) him

(C) them   (D) himself

翻譯

在典禮上,執行長親自頒獎給傑出員工。

(D)

9. She found _____ in a very awkward situation.

(A) her   (B) hers

(C) she   (D) herself

翻譯

她發現自己處於一個尷尬的處境。

(D) 她自己

10. My major is accounting, what is _____?

(A) your   (B) yours

(C) you   (D) yourself

翻譯

我主修會計，你呢？

(B) 你的

Unit 3 動詞

● 一、動詞的定義

　　動詞是用來表示各種的動作過程，依文法上的不同形式，動詞有以下不同的分類：

● 二、動詞的分類

※ 及物動詞 vs. 不及物動詞

1. 及物動詞

　　又分為：單及物動詞 & 雙及物動詞

　★ 單及物動詞：只有一個受詞的動詞

主詞 - 及物動詞 - 直接受詞

例句：

例 I love English.
　　我喜愛英語。

例 Nowadays many people read ebooks online.
　　現在很多人閱讀線上電子書。

★ 雙及物動詞：有兩個受詞的動詞

主詞 - 及物動詞 - 間接受詞 - 直接受詞

= 主詞 - 及物動詞 - 直接受詞 - 介系詞 - 間接受詞

請注意介系詞

例 Her mother gave her an English book.

= Her mother gave an English book to her.
她的母親給了她一本英文書。

例 My friend brought me a sandwich and a drink.

= My friend brought a sandwich and a drink for me.
我的朋友帶了一個三明治和一瓶飲料給我。

例 The teacher showed the students what they should practice.

例 = The teacher what they should practice to the students.
這位老師示範學生該做的練習給他們看。

2. 不及物動詞

例如：

例 I walk to school.
我走路上學。

例 Birds fly in the sky.
鳥在天上飛。

常見的不及物動詞包括：

※ 連綴動詞

◎ be 動詞：am, is, are, was, were, be, being, been

◎ 帶有助動詞的be 動詞：shall be, should be, can be, could be, will be, would be, may be, might be

◎ ......起來：look 看起來, smell 聞起來, sound 聽起來, taste 嚐起來, feel 覺得

◎ 似乎：seem 看似, appear 顯現

◎ 仍然： remain 仍然, stay 保持, keep 保持

◎ 變得： become 變成, grow 成為, turn 變成, go 變成, get 成為

例句：

例 Brian was very sad.
布萊恩很難過。

例 They remained silent.
他們保持沉默。

例 She looks fine.
她看起來很好。

例 The pork tastes sweet and sour.
這豬肉嚐起來酸酸甜甜的。

例 The flower smells great.
這花聞起來氣味真好。

※ 使役動詞

使役動詞 (causative verbs) 指的是驅使他人做某事的動詞，主要為：make, have, let...

其結構是：

使役動詞 ＋ 主事者 ＋ 原形動詞

例句：

例 Our English teacher makes us memorize 10 English words a day.
我們的英語老師要我們一天貝十個單字。

例 The school principle made the bully apologize to the victim.
我們校長要霸凌者向受害者道歉。

比較：

使役動詞 ＋ 受事者 ＋ V-en (過去分詞)

例句：I had my hair cut yesterday.

※ 感官動詞

感官動詞指表示感覺知能的動詞，主要為：

see 看見，watch 注視，hear 聽，feel 感覺，notice 注意，observe 觀察……

其結構是：

感官動詞 + 主事者 + 動詞原形或現在分詞

例句：

例 Did you happen to see anyone steal (stealing) in the shop?

你是否碰巧看見有誰在（正在）店裡偷東西呢？

例 At midnight, we heard a baby cry (crying) next door.

凌晨時我們聽見隔壁有嬰兒在（正在）哭。

使用現在分詞較動詞原形更強調此動作現在正在進行

比較：

感官動詞 + 受事者 + V-en (過去分詞)

例句：I saw him hit by a car.

※ 被動語態

1. 被動語態的定義

被動語態的作用被動語態是用來表示對「承受」某動作的人或物的關注，而不是關注「執行」某動作的人或物。換句話說，最重要的人或物變成句中的主詞。

★ 適合使用被動語態的情況

被動語態適合用於強調句中動作的受詞，有別於強調動作的執行者的主動語態。

例句：

例 Mark's invention was highly praised for its wide application in medical equipment.
馬克的發明因為可以大量用於醫療器材而廣受好評。

例 You can borrow the books if they are not ordered by someone online.
如果線上沒有別人預定的話，您就可以借這些書。

◎ 動作的行為者為泛指且不重要或顯而易見。

例句：

例 This medicine is taken before sleep (by patients).
這藥是睡前服用的。〔省略了病人〕

例 She was chosen as the winner (by the jury) in the Eurovision Song Contest this year.
她被選為今年歌唱大賽的得主。〔省略了評審團〕

◎ 被動語態用於轉述常理。

It is said that ... = people say ...

例句：

例 It is said that there is a will, there is a way.
常聽人說有志者事竟成。

It is believed that ... = people believe that ...

例句：

例 It was once believed that women were not capable of running for government.
從前婦女一度被認為沒有從政的能力。

　為了避免責任歸屬問題

2. 被動語態的構成

　　主動語態句子中的主詞於被動語態句子中變成 by + 受詞，或省略。

　　主動語態句子中的動詞於被動語態句子中變成 be + 過去分詞。

　　主動語態句子中的受詞於被動語態句子中變成主詞。

主動：名詞一　+　動詞 + 名詞二

被動：名詞二 +　be　+ 過去分詞　+　by　名詞一

例如：

主動：She loves him.　她愛他。

被動：--> He is loved by her.　他為她所愛。

主動：She loved him.　她愛過他。

被動：--> He was loved by her.　他曾為她所愛。

3. 被動語態的用法

◎ 句中有直接受詞與間接受詞時，直接受詞與間接受詞都可以當被動語態句子的主詞。

例如：

例 We gave him a room.
我們給他一間房間。

改為被動：

(1) A room was given to him by us.
一間房間由我們提供給他。
〔直接受詞作為主詞〕

(2) He was given a room by us.
他從我們這兒得到一間房間。
〔間接受詞作為主詞〕

◎否定句

　　(1) do not (did not) + 動詞 ==> be + not + 過去分詞

例如：

例 He did not call her.
他沒有打電話給她。

改被動--->

She was not called by him.
她沒有接到他的電話。

(2) 助動詞 + 動詞 ===> 助動詞 + not + be + 過去分詞

例如：

例 She cannot call him.
她不能打電話給他。

改被動--->

He cannot be called by her.
他不能接她的電話。

※ 時態

英語的時態非常嚴格，不僅經常會使用時間副詞點明時間點，動詞也必須要做變化與所對應的時態一致。

★ 時態共有以下幾類：

現在式、過去式、未來式
現在進行式、過去進行式、未來進行式
現在完成式、過去完成式、未來完成式
現在完成進行式、過去完成進行式、未來完成進行式

1. 現在式

現在式的形式

大部分動詞的現在式為動詞原形，第三人稱字尾要加上 -s, -es,

-ies；have的第三人稱為has；be動詞的現在式是am, are, is。

現在式適用情形

(1) 描述真理或事實。

No one is an island.
沒有人是一座孤島。

Silence is golden.
沉默是金。

(2) 描述現在的狀態或動作。

Laura is now divorced.
蘿拉目前是離婚狀態。

They are not rich, but always helpful to others.
他們雖不富有但總是樂於助人。

(3) 描述經常的習慣。

He gets up at 5:30 every morning.
他每天早上五點半起床。

Our boss never shows up at the office before noon.
我們老闆中午前不會到辦公室。

(4) 口語中表示預計將要發生的事。

Tomorrow is a public holiday.
明天是國定假日。

Next month our headquarter in Germany has a month off.
下個月我們位於德國的總公司休息一個月。

(5) 副詞子句中必須用現在式來代替未來式。

When I finish the research, I'll take a short break.
我完成研究後會短暫休息一下。

If the weather is nice tomorrow, we will go hiking.
如果明天天氣好的話，我們會去健行。

(6) 意思為「來、去」、「開始」的動詞常用現在式加上未來時間副詞表示未來。

go/come/leave/arrive/start ＋ tomorrow/next month/next year

Jason leaves here tomorrow evening.
傑森明天傍晚會離開這裡。

My work starts next Monday.
我的工作下星期一開始。

2. 過去式

過去式的形式

be動詞的過去式為was（am與is的過去式）；were（are的過去式）；其他動詞的過去式通常於字尾加上 -ed, -d，其餘為不規則變化過去式。

過去式適用情形

(1) 描述過去的狀態或動作

Back then he was not that interested in English.
那時候他還沒有對英語那麼有興趣。

In high school Rory developed a strong interest in reading science fictions.
在高中時羅里發展出閱讀科幻小說的強烈興趣。

(2) 描述過去的習慣

During high school, he borrowed at least 5 books a month from the city library.
高中時期他一個月至少向市立圖書館借五本書。

Whenever he had time, he would visit his parents living in the countryside.
只要他有時間就會去看住在鄉下的父母。

(3) 描述歷史

From 1895 to the end of World War II in 1945, Taiwan was a Japanese colony for 50 years.
從1895到1945年台灣是日本殖民地有五十年之久。

3. 未來式

未來式的形式

(1) will/shall ＋ Verb

(2) be going to ＋ Verb

未來式的形式是於原形動詞前加上will/shall 或 be going to。

未來式適用情形

(1) 描述未來發生的動作或狀態

◎ will ＋ Verb

These children will go on a hiking tour to the mountain in summer.
這些小孩在夏天會去山上健行。

Modern technology will develop at such a high speed that we cannot imagine.
現代科技會以我們無法想像的速度來發展下去。

◎ be going to + Verb

Are you going to study abroad after graduation?
畢業後你會去留學嗎？

Whatever is going to happen will happen, whether we worry or not. (Ana Monnar)
不論我們擔憂不擔憂，該發生的就是會發生。（安娜‧摩納）

(2) 表達說話者或聽者的意志，使用will, shall。

◎ will

I will finish the task as soon as I can.
我會儘快完成這項任務。

Love will conquer all.
愛會戰勝一切。

◎ shall

傳統原則：第一人稱代名詞（亦即I, we）與shall連用來形成未來式，其他的人稱代名詞（亦即you, he, she, it, they）則用will 來形成未來式，但是在現代英語中，通常一切人稱都習慣用will 。另外，如果要表達強烈的決心，則I, we 要與 will 連用。

Shall we dance?
我們一起跳舞吧？

We shall wait and see.
我們等著瞧。

Let's go, shall we?
我們一起走吧？

4. 現在進行式

現在進行式的形式

am/are/is ＋ V-ing

現在進行式是於be動詞的現在式（am/are/is）後加上現在分詞（V-ing）。

現在進行式適用情形

(1) 表示目前正在進行的動作

At this moment, almost all people are enjoying reunion dinner with their family members.
在這個時刻幾乎所有的人都在享受團圓飯。

The kettle is boiling.
水壺的水燒開了。

(2) 表示預計不久就要發生的動作，主要用於go, come, arrive, leave, start。

Our new secretary is coming tomorrow morning.
新秘書明天早上將會來到。

The bride and the bridegroom are starting a new chapter of life.
新娘和新郎正要開始人生新的一章。

5. 過去進行式

過去進行式的形式

was/were ＋ V-ing

過去進行式是於be動詞的過去式（was/were）後加上現在分詞（V-ing）。過去進行式表示過去某時刻正在進行的動作。

Judy was talking to someone on the phone when the doorbell rang.
門鈴響時茱蒂正在講電話。

When Matthew entered the room, everybody was too busy talking to notice him.
馬修進門時，每個人都忙著說話而沒注意到他。

6. 未來進行式

未來進行式的形式

will (shall) be ＋ V-ing

未來進行式是於be ＋ V-ing之前加上will (shall)，表示未來某時刻正在進行的動作。未來進行式表示某一行為會於未來某一時刻或某一時段進行。

Tomorrow morning, my husband will be receiving treatment from his dentist.
明天一早我先生要看牙醫。

We shall be landing New York in ten minutes.
我們十分鐘後會降臨紐約。

請特別注意：have, know 和感官動詞（feel, see, hear, notice）不可用於進行式。

7. 現在完成式

現在完成式的形式

have/has ＋ V-ed
現在完成式的形式為 have (has) 加上過去分詞。

現在完成式適用情形

(1) 表示從過去持續至現在的動作或狀態

Mary has played the piano for years, and she wants to be a piano teacher someday.
瑪莉彈鋼琴多年，她想要將來成為鋼琴老師。

Anderson has learned Japanese for quite some time since he started university.
自從開始唸大學以來，安德森已經學日語學了一段時間。

(2) 表示至今的經驗

Have you been to Japan?

You have made much progress in English learning.
你在英語學習上進步良多。

8. 過去完成式

過去完成式的形式

had ＋ V-ed

過去完成式的形式為 had 加上過去分詞。

過去完成式適用情形

(1) 表示於過去某一時刻之前已發生的動作

He had cleaned up the room when his mother got back home.
他母親回到家時，他已經將房間整理好。

No sooner had we arrived at the train station than our train left.
我們一到火車站，我們的火車就離開了。

〔no sooner 為否定詞，所以要倒裝〕

(2) 表示於過去某一時刻之前的經驗

Tim had never left his home country before he visited Japan.
在堤姆去日本前他從未出國過。

Before Ken became really fluent in English, he had tried many various methods of learning.
在肯恩的英語變得非常流利之前，他曾經試過很多不同的學習方式。

9. 未來完成式

未來完成式的形式

will (shall) have + V-ed

未來完成式的形式為 will (shall) have 加上過去分詞。未來完成式表示於未來某一時間之前已完成的動作或經驗。

By next June, they will have learned English for 5 years.
到了明年六月，他們學英語就有五年之久了。

Kent will have passed the exam when this summer arrives.
在今年夏天來臨時，肯特將已經通過考試。

10. 現在完成進行式

現在完成進行式的形式

have (has) been + V-ing

現在完成進行式的形式為 have(has) been 加上現在分詞。

現在完成進行式適用情形

現在完成進行式表示過去某時間開始的動作，通常還要再進行下去。

Jim has been watching TV the whole afternoon.
傑姆已經一整個下午都在看電視。

Since retirement, we have been living in the countryside.
自從退休後我們一直都住在鄉下。

11. 過去完成進行式

過去完成進行式的形式

had been + V-ing

過去完成進行式的形式為 had been 加上現在分詞。
過去完成進行式表示表示過去某時間開始的動作，通常持續到過去某一時刻。

Tom had been cooking before his girlfriend got back.

湯姆的女友回來前，他都在做飯。

Jill had been learning English in a wrong way before she met her current English teacher.

潔兒在遇見她目前的英文老師前，都是用一種錯誤方法在學英語。

12. 未來完成進行式

未來完成進行式的形式

will have been + V-ing

未來完成進行式的形式為 will have been 加上現在分詞。未來完成進行式表示動作於未來某時刻之前開始，持續至某時為止。

By next Autumn we will have been living in this district for 3 years.

到了下個秋天，我們就已經在這一地區住滿了三年。

The two brothers will have been studying in the school for one whole year by the end of this year.

到今年底為止，兩兄弟就會在這個學校上學滿一年了。

※ 常考：主詞與動詞的一致性

1. A and B

   A和B

   Mary and Terry are good friends.
   瑪莉與泰利是好朋友。

   Birth and death is part of life.
   生與死都是生命的一部分。（生與死為一體，故用單數動詞）

   Half of the students went on a trip.
   有一半的學生去郊遊了。

2. 表示時間、金錢、距離的複數名詞如果視為一個整體則用單數動詞，否則則用複數動詞。

   Two and half years is quite a long time.
   兩年半是相當長的一段時間。

   Five years have gone by, and Paul still has not finished his studies.
   五年已經過去了，保羅仍然還沒有完成學業。

1. **Hundreds and thousands of visitors _____ to this region by its magnificent landscape.**

    (A) are attracted　　　(B) attract

    (C) attracting　　　　(D) be attracted

詳解

　　此處要測驗的是被動語態，也就是be動詞後加上過去分詞，因為陳述的是事實，所以用現在式被動：are attracted。

翻譯

　　成千上萬的訪客被壯觀的地景給吸引到這裡來。

    (A) 被吸引

2. **She screamed upon _____ the thief took away her bag.**

    (A) sees　　　　　(B) seeing

    (C) saw　　　　　(D) had seen

詳解

　　介系詞upon/on後面要加上動名詞，所以這裡要用seeing。

翻譯

她一看見小偷在偷她袋子就尖叫起來。

(B) 看見

3. Please remember _____ this letter when you walk past the post office on your way to the office.

(A) to send   (B) sending

(C) sends   (D) have sent

詳解

記得要去做某件事，要用remember加不定詞，這裡的例子：remember to send（記得要去寄信）；記得做過某件事，則要用remember加動名詞：remember sending（記得寄過信）。

翻譯

請記得在上班途中經過郵局時，寄出這封信。

(A) 記得

4. Her grandmother could not remember _____ the question and kept asking it again and again.

(A) has asked   (B) having asked

(C) asked   (D) had asked

詳解

　　這裡的意思是「記得已經問過」，所以要用remember加上having asked（以過去完成式have asked改成動名詞而成）。

翻譯

　　她的祖母無法忘記問過這個問題，一直重複問。

　　(B) 問過

5. Kevin gave his _____ laptop to his friend because his mother gave him a new one.

　　(A) uses　　　　　　(B) using

　　(C) is used　　　　　(D) used

詳解

　　此處依句意需要的是由過去分詞來當形容詞，表示用過的，也就是二手的，所以選used。

翻譯

　　凱文將他用過的筆電送給他的朋友，因為他的母親送了一台新的給他。

　　(D) 用過的

6. **By this time of next year, I _____ for 10 years for this company.**

(A) am working　　　(B) worked

(C) will have worked　(D) working

詳解

　　因為 By this time of next year（到明年的這個時候），這個副詞片語，知道需要使用未來完成式的時態，

will have worked（會已經工作），表示這個時間點之前。

翻譯

　　到明年的這個時候，我就會在這公司服務了十年。

(C) 會已經工作

7. **The students _____ their group discussions by the time the teacher asked them to stop.**

(A) had finished　　(B) have finished

(C) having finished　(D) finish

詳解

　　因為句中 asked 為 ask（要求）的過去式，所以要用過去完成式，表示這個時間點之前。

翻譯

　　老師要學生們停止時，他們已經完成了小組討論

(A) 已經完成了

8. It's so _____ to bake after computer work.

(A) relax   (B) relaxed

(B) relaxes   (D) relaxing

詳解

這裡依句意需要的是relax（放鬆）的現在分詞relaxing來當作形容詞。

翻譯

做完電腦工作後來烘焙，真是令人放鬆啊。

(D) 令人放鬆

9. If I _____ hard at that time, I would have got the promotion.

(A) worked   (B) had worked

(C) have worked   (D) working

詳解

因為有at that time（那時），所以要用與過去事實相反的假設法。

翻譯

要是我那時努力工作，我可能就會得到升遷了。

(B) 曾經努力工作

10. _____ somewhere else fishing, will you?

(A) Going   (B) Go

(C) Goes   (D) Gone

詳解

這裡要用祈使句來表達 一種命令。

翻譯

你去別的地方釣魚好嗎？

(B) 去

U n i t

4 形容詞

●一、形容詞的定義

修飾名詞的詞稱為形容詞。

1. 形容詞的位置

A. 前位修飾：形容詞位於所修飾的名詞片語之前，例如：a clever boy（一個聰明的男孩）；後位修飾：形容詞位於所修飾的名詞片語之後，通常用於修飾語較長，大於一個單詞時，例如：a boy clever as you（一個像你這樣聰明的男孩）。

有些複合詞固定要用後位修飾，特別是法律相關名詞，例如：

the authorities concerned 有關當局

the president-elect 總統當選人

the secretary general 秘書長

a professor emeritus 名譽教授

B. 修飾複合不定代名詞時，要用後位修飾，例如：

anybody interesting 任何有意思的人

anything new 任何新的事

everybody present 在場的所有人

everything related to Japan 所有與日本相關的事

someone special 某個特別的人

something boring 某件無聊的事

nothing meaningful 沒有任何有意義的事

●二、形容詞的特別用法

1. the ＋ 形容詞 ＝ 具有此形容詞特質的一群人（通常為複數）。

the rich 有錢人

the poor 貧窮的人

the weak 弱者

the unemployed 失業的人

比較：

the ＋ 某抽象觀念的形容詞（通常為單數）

例如：

the true 真，the good 善，the beautiful 美

2. 分詞形容詞

A. 現在分詞：V-ing，意思為主動，未完成，例如：interesting project 有意思的企劃案，smoking house 冒煙的房子。

B. 過去分詞：V-ed，意思為被動，已完成，例如：feel interested 感到有興趣，smoked sausage 煙燻的香腸。

●三、形容詞的種類

形容詞的種類主要分為：

A. 性質形容詞，例如：big 大的，small 小的，tall 高的，happy 高興的，positive 正面思考的⋯⋯

B. 顏色形容詞，例如：red 紅的，yellow 黃的，green 綠的⋯⋯

C. 類別形容詞，例如：golden 黃金的，wooden 木製的，artificial 人工的，medicinal 藥用的⋯⋯

◎類別形容詞原則上沒有比較級、最高級。

例如：

a special green medicinal plant 一種特殊綠色可作藥用的植物

a beautiful red artificial flower 一種美麗的紅色人造花

the big yellow wooden doll 一個大型的黃色木製人偶

構造上還有複合形容詞：cold-blooded 冷血的，single-handed 單手的，well-prepared 準備充分的⋯⋯

● 四、形容詞的比較級和最高級

1. 形容詞的等級(degree) 可以用比較級和最高級來表示：

原級：形容詞的原來形式。

比較級：兩個人或物當中做比較時，要用形容詞的比較級形式。

最高級：三個或三個以上的人或物當中做比較時，要用形容詞的最高級形式。

2. 形容詞比較級和最高級的形成

A. 單音節的形容詞，加上 er，形成比較級，加上 est，形成最高級。

B. 三個或三個以上音節的形容詞，前面加上 more，形成比較級，前面加上 most，形成最高級。

C. 字尾是 e 時，加上 r 時形成比較級，加上 st，形成最高級。

D. 字尾為子音字母加 y 者，先去掉 y，再加上 ier，形成比較級，加上 iest，形成最高級。

E. 字尾為母音字母加 y 者，加上 er，形成比較級，加上 est，形成最高級。

F. 字尾為 ed, en, ing, ly 者，前面加上 more，形成比

較級，前面加上most，形成最高級。

G. 有些形容詞沒有比較級與最高級，因為是絕對的概念，例如：correct 正確的， horizontal水平的，parallel平行的，perfect 完美的，right 正確的，round 圓的 straight直的，vertical 垂直的，wrong 錯誤的……

H. 前面加上 more，形成正向比較級，前面加上most，形成正向最高級；相對而言，前面加上less，形成負向比較級，前面加上least，形成負向最高級。

I. 不規則形容詞的變化

bad/ill -- worse -- worst 壞的--更壞--最壞的

good/well -- better -- best 好的--更好--最好的

little -- less -- least 少--更少--最少

many/much -- more -- most 多--更多--最多

常見不規則形容詞的變化表

原級	字意	比較級	最高級
good well	好的 健康的， 很好地	better	best
bad ill badly	壞的 有病的 拙劣地	worse	worst
many much	許多	more	most
little	少許的	less	least
old	老的、舊的	older elder	oldest eldest
late	遲的 後者的	later latter	latest last
far	遠的 遠的、更多， 更進一步	farther further	farthest furthest

3. 表示比較的常用語

※ 原級

◎ as 原級 as　與……一樣……

This suitcase is as expensive as that one over there.
這個行李箱跟那邊的那個一樣貴。

◎ not as (so) 原級　as　不像……一樣……

Her health is not so good as before.
她的健康不若從前那麼好。

◎ more/less 原級 than　比……更……

In the meeting I was less talkative than Jennifer.
開會時我說的話比珍妮佛少。

※ 比較級

◎ 比較級 + than　比……還……

Alice is more reliable and trustworthy than any other employees in the office.
愛麗絲比辦公室裡的其他員工都還要可靠，值得信賴。

◎ 比較級 + and + 比較級 (more and more 三音節和以上的形容詞原級) 越來越……

This medicine has become darker and darker.
這藥越變越暗。

If you do not learn English grammar step by step, it can get more and more difficult.
如果你不按步就班學習英文文法，就會越來越難學會。

◎ the 比較級...... ＋ the 比較級......　　越......就越......

The more I learn English, the easier it becomes.
我越學英語，英語就變得越簡單。

The more I practice playing the guitar, the more fun I get from it.
我越練習，彈吉他就越來越有意思。

◎ all the 比較級　更加......

Welcome to bring friends with you to the dinner. The more people are all the better.
歡迎帶朋友來參加晚宴，越多人越好。

The English grammar has become all the more difficult since this semester.
英文文法從這學期以來就變得越來越難。

◎ no 比較級 (than) 不會更......

His position is no better than a secretary.
他在公司裡的職位與秘書差不多。

◎ **what is 比較級 更......的是**

What is better, you won a free return ticket to Seoul.
更好的是，你贏得了首爾免費來回機票。

What is worse, he often acts as if he were the boss.
更糟的是，他經常表現得像個老闆似的。

◎ **後接介系詞 to 的比較級**

● **inferior to** 不如的，下級的

She has self-confidence and never feels inferior to anybody.
她自信心很充足，從來不覺得比不上任何人。

● **junior to** 年輕的，資位較低的

Kelly might be junior to you in age, but please treat her like any other new employees in the company.
雖然凱莉可能年紀上比你們小，但是請將她視為跟公司其他新進人員一樣。

● **senior to** 年長的，資位較高的

Although he is senior to all of us, he is always very humble and helpful.
雖然他的資位比我們的都高，但是他總是非常謙虛且樂於助人。

※ 最高級

◎ 最高級...... ＋ 介系詞片語

He is the most responsible employee in the company.
他是公司裡最負責任的員工。

This is perhaps the hardest problem I have ever encountered in my work.
這或許是我工作遇過最難的問題。

◎ one of the ＋ 最高級　　當中最......

One of the most challenging tasks is to work in a team made of people from various cultural backgrounds.
當中最有挑戰性的是，在一個由不同文化背景組成的團隊裡工作。

One of the hardest things is to have to deal with people you have hurt before.
最難的是必須要跟你曾經傷害過的人相處。

◎ almost 幾乎，by far 遠超過於，nearly 幾乎， second 第二個（序數），very 非常...... ＋ 最高級

James' design of architecture is by far the most creative among all the contestants.
詹姆斯的建築設計是所有參賽者當中最有創意的。

五、相同屬性的才能比較

相同屬性的形容詞或副詞才能比較

◆ 正確

The buildings in Taipei are older than those in Tokyo.

◆ 常見錯誤

The buildings in Taipei are older than Tokyo.

牛刀小試 ►TEST

1. This new assistant is just as _____ as the previous one.

    (A) most capable   (B) less capable

    (C) more capable   (D) capable

詳解

    句中as……as這個片語表示與什麼一樣，所以要用形容詞原形。

翻譯

    這個新助理就像之前的助理那樣能幹。

    (D) 能幹

2. This doll is much _____ beautiful than the other one.

    (A) more   (B) less

    (C) most   (D) least

詳解

    因為句中有than所以要用形容詞的比較級，表示前者比後者更據有某種特質。

翻譯

    這個洋娃娃比另外一個還要更漂亮。

    (A) 更

3. Jason is a _____ worker and he deserves a pay raise.

(A) hardly   (B) harder

(C) hard   (D) hardest

詳解

此處要用hard（認真的）來形容worker（工人），而hardly為副詞，表示幾乎不。

翻譯

傑森是個認真的工人，他值得加薪。

(C) 認真的

4. Of all the employees here, the boss thinks Ted is the _____ one.

(A) better   (B) best

(C) good   (D) worse

詳解

因為句子開端就指出，在所有這裡的員工中，所以要使用最高級。

翻譯

這裡的員工中，老闆認為泰德是最頂尖的。

(B) 最佳的

5. There is no _____ road to success.

(A) long   (B) flat

(C) royal   (D) hard

詳解

這裡需要一個形容詞來修飾後面的名詞 road（道路），選項皆為形容詞：(A) 長的；(B) 平的；(D) 硬的，皆與句意不符，刪去之後，只有(C) 皇家的，可以放在這裡，這是一句諺語，意思是：沒有通往成功的王道，也就是成功沒有捷徑。

翻譯

成功沒有捷徑。

(C) 皇家的

6. Forgiveness is one of the _____ lessons to learn in life.

(A) hardest   (B) harder

(C) more hard   (D) most hard

詳解

在這裡選項皆是由形容詞 hard 變化而來，hard 的比較級是 harder，最高級是 hardest，並沒有 more hard ，most hard 的用法，而這裡有 one of the… ，所以後面要用最高級，所以正確為 hardest。

翻譯

原諒是人生中最難的功課之一。

(A) 最難的

7. This assignment is _____ time-consuming than what I used to be given before.

(A) most   (B) much more

(C) least   (D) so

詳解

因為句中有than，所以要用比較級，這裡只有 (B) 是比較級，而在前面加上much，則是表示「更為」。

翻譯

這份任務比我之前的任務來得耗時得多。

(B) 耗時得多

8. Don't be afraid to ask her out. The _____ result you could get is a polite refusal.

(A) good   (B) worse

(C) better   (D) worst

詳解

此處根據句意，這裡空格處應該要表示「最糟糕的」的意思，所以選(D) worst（最壞的）。

翻譯

不要怕約她出去，最糟糕的結果你會得到的是有禮的拒絕。

(D) worst　最壞的

9. The actress is not only good-looking but also
   _____. She always donates money to charity
   groups.

(A) warmer heart (B) warm-heart

(C) warmest heart (D) warm-hearted

詳解

這裡 not only……but also……，必須要用同樣的詞性，good-looking是形容詞（好看的），所以要選用選項中唯一的形容詞warm-hearted（心地好的）。

翻譯

這位女演員不但漂亮而且心地善良，她總是捐錢給慈善團體。

(D) 心地善良的

10. Our _____ computer in the office saves us lots
    of time.

(A) multitask (B) multitasking

(C) multiple (D) multitasker

詳解

　　要修飾computer（電腦），所以需要一個形容詞，而選項 (A) multitask（多工），(D) multitasker（多工者），兩者皆為名詞；(C) multiple（多數的），(B) multitasking（多工的），兩者為形容詞，根據句意，只有 (B) 符合。

翻譯

我們辦公室多工的電腦，為我們節省不少時間。

(B) 多工的

Unit 5 副詞

●一、副詞的定義

副詞是用來修飾動詞、形容詞、其它副詞，或是整句的詞類。

●二、詞的構成

大部分副詞為形容詞字尾加上ly 而形成，例如：efficient（有效率的）字尾加上ly變成efficiently（有效率地）。

●三、副詞的種類

1. 時間副詞

tomorrow 明天，yesterday 昨天，then 那時候，before 之前， after 之後，soon 很快地，later 後來，at first 起先……

例句：

例 Yesterday Jack got back from his trip to Canada.
昨天傑克從加拿大旅遊回來。

例 After sunset, they felt hungry and started to look for a restaurant.
太陽西下後他們感到餓了，便開始尋找餐廳。

2. 頻率副詞

always 總是，often 經常地，frequently 經常地，seldom 很少地，rarely 幾乎不，never 不曾……

例句：

例 Kelly always has a yearly health check-up in the beginning of a year.
凱莉總是在年初做年度健康檢查。

例 Johnathan usually tries to solve his problems by himself.
強納森通常獨自解決問題。

◎ 如果句子是以否定的副詞開始，則需要倒裝，請見以下的例句：

例 Never would I think of hurting others or stealing things.
我從來不曾想過要傷害他人或偷東西。

例 Seldom did Frank take sick leave in school.
法蘭克幾乎不曾請病假。

3. 地點副詞

here 這裡，there 那裡，down 下面，up 上面，near 靠近，out 外面……

例句：

例 There came one tourist asking for directions.
那邊有個觀光客走來問路。

例 Please don't get close to that red car.
請不要接近那輛紅色的車。

4. 方式副詞

hard 努力地，well 好地，fast 快速地，quickly 很快地，gently 溫柔地，rudely 粗魯地，briefly 簡短地，roughly 大略地……

例句：

例 Let me briefly explain the schedule for you.
讓我為你簡短地解釋一下時間表。

例 The doctor listens to his patients carefully.
這位醫師很仔細地聆聽病人。

5. 程度副詞

very 很，so 如此，much 非常，enough 夠，little 有點，really 真地， absolutely 絕對地，exactly 正是，entirely 全然地，completely 完全地⋯⋯

例句：

例 After the earthquake, this place was completely damaged.
地震後這個地方全毀了。

例 Don't believe what he said to you entirely.
不要完全相信他所說的話。

6. 否定副詞

no 沒有，not 沒有的，never 不曾，seldom 很少地，hardly 幾乎沒有地，rarely 非常少地⋯⋯

例句：

例 There has seldom been such talented musician in our community.
在我們社區很少有這樣有天賦的音樂家。

例 This restaurant was so noisy that we could hardly hear each other.
這家餐廳是如此吵雜，以至於我們幾乎聽不見對方的聲音。

◎ 如果句子是以否定的副詞開始，則需要倒裝。

例句：

例 Never have I been late with my homework.
我從來不曾遲交過作業。

例 Rarely does she travel overseas.
她很少出國旅遊。

7. 不定副詞

somewhere 某地，sometime 某時，somehow 不知怎麼地，everywhere 到處……

例句：

例 Let's catch up with each other sometime.
我們找個時間來敘舊。

例 Somehow I have to talk him into giving up smoking.
無論如何我都必須說服他戒菸。

8. 全句副詞

generally 大致來說，fortunately 幸運地，unfortunately 不幸地，apparently 很明顯地，honestly 老實說……

例句：

例 Honestly, this apartment costs far more than we can afford.
老實說這間公寓遠超過我們能負擔的範圍。

例 Unfortunately, he passed away this time last year.
不幸地，他在去年的這個時候過世了。

9. 連接副詞

therefore 如此一來，nevertheless 然而，furthermore 再者，consequently 因此……

例句：

例 Most models are skinny; therefore, many young people become obsessive about losing weight.
大部分模特兒都是皮包骨，因此很多年輕人瘋狂減重。

例 Quite a few young people have no knowledge of nutrition; furthermore, they live under huge stress.
很多年輕人沒有營養知識，還有，他們的生活充滿壓力。

10. 焦點副詞

almost 大多，just 剛好，nearly 幾乎，only 唯一……

例句：

例 In the past almost all graduates from this department wanted to work for the government.
在過去，幾乎所有系上畢業生都想要在公家單位工作。

例 It will all work out just fine.
一切都會沒問題的。

● 四、副詞的位置

　　副詞通常放於所修飾的動詞、形容詞、副詞附近，修飾整句時通常放於句首。

They say he is somewhat eccentric.
他們說他有點神經質。

Fortunately, we finished all the tasks before due date, and everyone was pleased.
幸運的是，我們在截止日期前完成了所有任務，大家都很滿意。

Generally speaking, most employees here do not work more than two year in this company.
一般說來，這裡大部分員工不會在這家公司待超過兩年。

● 五、與形容詞同形的副詞

※ better 更好

例句：

作形容詞：This tea tastes better than that one. 這種茶嚐起來比那種好。

作副詞：The assistant works better than the previous

one. 這位助理做得比前一位好。

※ deep 深

例句：

作形容詞：The water of this pond is very deep. 這池塘非常深。

作副詞：Don't get deep in the well. 不要到這水井的深處去。

※ extra 多餘

例句：

作形容詞：Do you have extra money to lend me? 你有多的錢借我嗎？

作副詞：He works extra hard to get a promotion. 他為了獲得升遷而格外努力工作。

※ fast 快

例句：

作形容詞：He is a fast eater. 他吃東西吃得很快。

作副詞：He walks usually very fast. 他走路通常很快。

※ first 首先

例句：

作形容詞：He is the first person to get a raise in this company. 他是這家公司裡第一個得到升遷的人。

作副詞：Finish your meal first before watching TV. 先吃完飯再看電視。

※ high 高

例句：

作形容詞：She got a high score in ice skating. 她在溜冰項目中獲得高分。

作副詞：Don't climb so high! 不要爬那麼高。

※ last 最後

例句：

作形容詞：Even on her last day, she still worked very hard. 即使是最後一天，她仍然很努力工作。

作副詞：Finish your meal first, and eat the dessert last. 先吃完飯，最後再吃甜點。

※ late 遲

例句：

作形容詞：Do not hand in late assignments. 不要遲交作業。

作副詞：This morning he got up very late. 他今早很遲才起床。

※ next 下個

例句：

作形容詞：Take the next train. 搭下班火車。

作副詞：She first watched the film and read the novel next. 她先看電影然後才看原著小說。

六、形容詞加上 ly，變成意義不同的副詞

※ late

◆ **late**
形容詞：遲到的

You are late again. 你又遲到了。

◆ **lately**
副詞：最近

Have you seen him lately? 你最近是否看到過他？

※ hard

◆ **hard** 作形容詞：艱難的
This is a hard task. 這是個艱辛的任務。

◆ **hard** 作副詞：辛苦地
He has worked very hard to get to this position. 他非常努力工作才能得到這個職位。

◆ **hardly**
副詞：幾乎沒有，幾乎不

There was hardly any female medical student at that time. 那個時候幾乎沒有任何女生讀醫學系。

＃特殊

◆ **pretty**

作形容詞：美麗的

She is a pretty girl. 她是個美麗的女孩。

作副詞：非常地

She looks pretty young for her age.

她看起來比實際年紀年輕。

七、需要注意的副詞片語

1.

◆ **not...any longer=no longer** 不再

例句：

例 He could not put up with it any longer.

= He could no longer put up with it.
他沒辦法再忍受了。

◆ **not...anymore =no more** 不再

例句：

例 He could not work there anymore.

= He could work there no more.
他不再能夠在那裡工作了。

2.

◆ **not more than=at most** 至多

例句

例 I cannot pay you more than 500 dollars.

= I can pay you 500 dollars at most.
我最多可以付500元給你。

◆ **not less than=at least** 至少

例句：

例 This house would not cost less than 8 million dol-lars.

= This house would cost at least 8 million dollars.
這間房子至少值八百萬元。

3.

◆ **no more than=only** 僅僅

例句：

例 Right now I have no more than 1500 dollars with me.

= Right now I have only 1500 dollars with me.
現在我身上僅有1500元。

4.

no less than=as much as 有……那麼多（通常表示多的意思）

例句：

例 She has no less than 5,500,000 dollars.

= She has as much as 5,500,000 dollars.

她有550萬元那麼多錢。

 牛刀小試
▶TEST

1. The accountant comes in the office _____ only when the boss needs the accounting service.

(A) occasionally　　(B) always

(C) never　　(D) often

詳解

這裡要選的是最正確的頻率副詞，句意是「只有在……」的時候，所以要選 (A) occasionally有時候。而其他選項的意思分別是 (B) always 總是，(C) never 從不，(D) often 經常。

翻譯

這位會計只有時在老闆需要會計服務時進辦公室。

(A) 有時

2. I do not like to go to a farewell party because it is not easy to say good-bye _____.

(A) carelessly　　(B) properly

(C) late　　(D) verbal

詳解

這裡需要的是副詞，(A) carelessly 草率地，(B) properly妥當地，(C) late 遲地，句意是指「好好說再見」，所以正確答案為 (B) 。而 (D) verbal則為形容詞，意思

是口頭上的。

翻譯

我不喜歡去參加餞別，因為要好好說再見很不容易。

(B) 妥善地

3. Susan _____ calls anything a failure. For her, everything is a learning experience.

(A) frequently   (B) often

(C) always   (D) never

詳解

根據句意，(D) never 從不，是最適合的頻率副詞。其它 (A) frequently 經常，(B) often 常常，(C) always 總是。

翻譯

蘇珊從來不會將任何事稱為失敗，對她而言，每件事都是可學習的經驗。

(D) 從來不會

4. Jason has to study _____ than before in order to pass the final exam.

(A) more diligently   (B) not diligently

(C) most diligently   (D) less diligently

詳解

　　句中有 than before，所以要用比較級，表示「比之前還來得更……」，所以答案為 (A) 更努力。

翻譯

　　傑森必須要更努力學習，才能通過期末考。

　　(A) 更努力學習

---

5. Why don't we meet up with each other _____ next week?

　　(A) sometimes　　　　(B) sometime

　　(C) some time　　　　(D) some of time

詳解

　　句意是指下周某個時間，所以答案為 (B) sometime。其它選項為 (A) sometimes 有時候，(C) some time 一些時間，(D) some of time 時間中一部分。

翻譯

　　下星期我們何不找個時間來碰面？

　　(B) 某個時間

---

6. The _____ you learn English, the more fun it brings you.

　　(A) less　　　　　　(B) most

　　(C) more　　　　　　(D) much

詳解

　　"The more……, the more……" 句型結構表示中文的「越……，就越……」，這裡的the more可以用比較級形容詞或副詞。

翻譯

　　你英文學習越久，英文就會帶給你越多樂趣。

　　(C) 更

7. My brain functions ＿＿＿＿＿ in the early morning after I just get up.

(A) efficient

(B) more efficient

(C) most efficient

(D) most efficiently

詳解

　　這裡的function當作動詞，表示運作的意思，因此需要一個副詞來修飾，選項中只有(D) most efficiently 為副詞，表示最為有效率地，所以是正確選項。

翻譯

　　我的頭腦在我一早起來運作最有效率。

　　(D) 最有效率地

8. One can ＿＿＿＿＿ tell it is a fake Rolex watch.

(A) hard

(B) hardly

(C) easy

(D) easier

詳解

　　這裡根據句意需要一個副詞來修飾動詞 tell（分辨），而選項中只有 (B) hardly（幾乎不能）符合句意。其它答案 (A) hard 作副詞是努力地，作形容詞是堅硬的；(C) easy 是形容詞，容易的，(D) easier 則是比較級，更容易的。

翻譯

　　這勞力士假錶看起來幾乎像真的。

　　(B) 幾乎

9. Thank you for help me this time. You are _____ a friend to me.

(A) very　　　　　　(B) sure

(C) best　　　　　　(D) quite

詳解

　　在這裡要表示「真的」，而且要在 a friend（一個朋友）之前，英文要用副詞 quite（相當地），其它都不合。

翻譯

　　謝謝你這次幫我忙，你真的是我的好朋友。

　　(D) 真的是

10. He is old _____ to vote this in the coming election.

(A) too   (B) enough

(C) much   (D) less

詳解

英文要表示某個形容詞的質量「足夠」，要在形容詞這裡是old（年老的），後面加上enough，表示「夠老的」。

翻譯

這次選舉他符合年紀資格可以投票。

(B) 足夠

U n i t 6 介系詞

●一、介系詞的作用

　　置於名詞或代名詞（受格）前面，構成形容詞性介系詞片語修飾名詞，或副詞性介系詞片語修飾動詞、形容詞、副詞。

1. 形容詞性介系詞片語

例句：

例 The jewelry in the box is gone.
這個盒子裡的珠寶不見了。

2. 副詞性介系詞片語

例句：

例 He put the money into the red envelop.
他將錢放進紅包袋裡。

●二、介系詞的種類

1. 表示地點與方向的介系詞

※ 在什麼地方的介系詞

　　表示在某個地方通常用"in"；若是地點較小，為某一特定地點則用"at"；若是在某地點上方則用"on"。

◆ **in**　在某個較大地點

例 As time went by, he felt more and more at home living in a big city.
隨著時間過去，他感到越來越習慣住在大城市。

◆ **at**　在某個較小地點

例 We met each other at a language school.
我們是在一間語言學校認識的。

◆ **on**　在某地點上方

例 Have you been on the top of Taipei 101?
你曾經到過台北101頂端嗎？

※ 在什麼地方之正上方、之正下方的介系詞

◆ **over**　在什麼地方之正上方

例 He planted orange trees all over his farm.
他在農場上種滿了柳丁樹。

◆ **under**　在什麼地方之正下方

例 They are having a picnic under cherry flowers.
他們在櫻花下野餐。

※ 在什麼地方上方、下方的介系詞

◆ **above**　在什麼地方之上方

例 Above the mountain, there is a statue.
在山頂上有座雕像。

◆ **below**　在什麼地方之下方

例 Do you like the oil painting below this drawing?
你喜歡這素描下方的油畫嗎？

補充：

我們使用over表示在某物正上方，under表示在某物正下方；above表示在某物上方範圍，below表示在某物下方範圍，因此可知用over的情形也可用above來描述，用under的情形也可用below來描述。

※ 表示地點的介系詞：in front of、behind

◆ **in front of**　在……之前

例 In the line there were 13 people standing in front of me.
排隊隊伍中有13個人排在我前面。

◆ **behind**　在……之後

例 Do you know the guy sitting behind you?
你認得在坐在你後面的人嗎？

※ 表示地點的介系詞：near、against、inside、outside

◆ **near**　靠近

例 There are many pine trees near the house.
靠近屋子處種了很多松樹。

◆ **against**　靠著

例 Tom leaned against the wall for support.
湯姆靠著牆支撐身體。

◆ **inside**　在……之內

例 Most people are afraid of going inside the haunted house.
大部分人都不敢進入這間鬼屋。

◆ **outside**　在……之外

例 Please wait for us outside the gallery.
請在藝廊外面等我們。

※ **表示相對位置的介系詞：opposite、between、among**

◆ **opposite**　在……對面

例 The sales manager sat opposite to me during the meeting.

◆ **between**　在……之間（兩者之間）

例 There are some low trees between the two houses.
兩個屋子間種了些小樹。

例 The two sisters decided to share the food between themselves.
這兩姊妹決定兩個人來分享食物。

◆ **among** 在……之間（三者或三者以上）

例 The teacher always sits among his students in class.
那位老師上課時喜歡和學生坐在一起。

例 Among all students in the class, Amy did best in her research paper.
在班上所有學生當中，艾美的研究報告寫得最好。

※ **進出什麼地方的介系詞：into、out of**

◆ **into** 進入

例 We have never walked into the forest.
我們從來沒有進入這座森林過。

◆ **out of** 出來

例 Out of nowhere, a shadow suddenly appeared.
一個黑影突然冒出來了。

※ **表示沿著或穿過的介系詞：along、across、over**

◆ **along** 沿著

例 We enjoy walking along the river after dinner.
我們喜歡於晚飯後沿著河岸散步。

◆ **across** 穿過

例 When walking across street, you should pay attention to the coming cars.
穿越馬路時要注意來車。

◆ **over** 過

例 Go over the bridge and you will see us.
走過橋就可以看見我們。

※ 表示向上，向下的介系詞：up、down

◆ **up** 向上

例 He went up to the mountain almost every morning.
幾乎每天早上他都去山上。

◆ **down** 向下

例 The teacher has never come down from the podium.
那個老師不曾從講台走下來。

※ 前往或離開某地點的介系詞：from、to、for

◆ **from** 從什麼地方離開

例 The flight from Tokyo to Taipei was delayed for almost 1 hour.
從東京到台北的班機延誤了將近一小時。

◆ **to** 前往什麼地方

例 He decided to fly to Tokyo to have a meeting with the client in person.
他決定飛往東京去與一位客戶親自會面。

◆ **for** 前往什麼地方

例 He left for Korea for skiing.
他前往韓國滑雪。

2. 表示時間的介系詞

※ 於什麼時間的介系詞

◆ **in**

例 The lucky winner will be drawn in this week.
幸運得主會於本週抽出。

◆ **on**

例 On Friday, many staff leave early in this company.
星期五很多員工都提早離開公司。

◆ **at**

例 He always finishes his work at sharp 5 pm.
他總是下午五點準時下班。

※ 於什麼時間之前或之後的介系詞

◆ **before** 於什麼時間之前

例 All tasks have to be finished before the deadline.
所有的任務都要在截止期限之前完成。

◆ **after** 於什麼時間之後

例 No garbage will be collected after 18:00.
18:00後不會收任何垃圾。

※ 有一段時間的介系詞

◆ **for** 有一段時間

例 I have known this young salesman for almost 5 years.
我認識這個年輕的業務專員已經有五年之久。

◆ **during** 在什麼期間

例 During your stay here, you can always stay at our place.
你待在這裡的期間都可以住在我們家。

※ 直到什麼時間的介系詞

◆ **until** 直到

例 People often do not cherish something until it is lost.
人們通常直到失去才懂得珍惜。

◆ **by** 最遲什麼時候

例 By this time of next year, I'd like to be able to buy a new house.
到明年的這個時候，我希望能夠買間新房子。

3. 其它介系詞

※ 由什麼製成

◆ **be made of** 物理變化（本質不變）

例 The desk is made of wood.
這個桌子是木材做的。

◆ **be made from** 化學變化（本質已變）

例 The wine is made from organic grape.
這個酒是有機葡萄做的。

※ with & without

◆ **with** 帶有

例 We went home with many sweets.
我們帶了很多甜點回家。

◆ **without** 沒有

例 Without her help, we could not have finished the
project.
如果沒有她的幫忙，我們不可能完成這個企劃案。

1. She seems to be interested _____ the vacant position.

(A) of   (B) at

(C) in   (D) to

詳解

根據句意要使用be interested in來表示對於某件事，後面要接名詞。

翻譯

她似乎對空出的職缺感到有興趣。

(C) 對於

2. Your previous boss speaks highly _____ you.

(A) on   (B) at

(C) for   (D) of

詳解

根據句意要使用speak highly of來表示對某人讚譽有加，後面加上某人。

翻譯

你的前老闆對你讚譽有佳。

(D) 對於

3. They regard their boss _____ a motherly figure for her leadership and kindness.

(A) for   (B) on

(C) at   (D) as

詳解

這裡已經有了regard，因此要加上as來表示將什麼人事物視為什麼。

翻譯

他們將他們的老闆視為母親，這是因為她的領導能力和仁慈。

(D) 當作

4. _____ far as I am concerned, this business is in danger and cannot be profitable in the industry.

(A) For   (B) As

(C) Yet   (D) At

詳解

就誰來說或就誰而言，可以用as far as somebody is concerned表示，後面接著的是某人的意見或看法。

翻譯

就我而言，這個生意很危險，在業界無法獲利。

(B) 就，針對

5. He has not contacted his parents _____ a long time since he moved out.

(A) on   (B) at

(C) of   (D) for

詳解

完成式經常要用for來接著表示一段時間的名詞，表示已經有一段時間都持續某個動作或狀態。

翻譯

自從搬出家後，他已經很久沒有聯絡他的父母了。

(D) 很久的介系詞

6. The music department _____ this school is very famous around the country.

(A) of   (B) on

(C) about   (D) around

詳解

要用介系詞of來表示「屬於」的意思，這裡是指這個學校的音樂系。

翻譯

這所學校的音樂系很有名。

(A) 屬於的介系詞

7. It's no use crying _____ spilled milk.

(A) with (B) over

(C) of (D) to

詳解

　　介系詞over表示因為什麼的原因。這也是一句諺語，意思是後悔無法改變的事，一點也沒有用。

翻譯

　　覆水難收。

　　(B) 關於何事

8. All of us look forward _____ traveling to Japan with a professional guide.

(A) at (B) to

(C) over (D) toward

詳解

　　表示期待，經常用look forward to這個片語，要注意的是之後要加名詞或動名詞。

翻譯

　　我們都很期待跟專業導遊一起去日本旅行。

　　(B) 對某事期待

9. I'd like to talk to the person who is in charge _____ the store here.

(A) at   (B) over

(C) for   (D) of

詳解

負責某間公司或店家，常用Somebody is in charge of something。

翻譯

我想跟負責這家商店的人談話。

(D) in chage of 負責

10. An infant car seat can prevent babies _____ having accidents.

(A) from   (B) over

(C) of   (D) until

詳解

表示防止某人發生某事常用prevent somebody from something，介系詞要用from，後面要接名詞或動名詞。

翻譯

嬰兒椅可以防止嬰兒發生意外。

(A) 防止某事的介系詞

Unit 7 連接詞

● 一、連接詞的定義

連接詞是用來連接相同詞類與子句的詞類。

● 二、連接詞的分類

1. 對等連接詞：分為單詞對等連接詞 & 片語對等連接詞

單詞對等連接詞：

and 然而，but 但是，or 或，yet 卻，for 因為，so 所以……

※ and 和，而且

連接對等詞類

All staff members, new and old ones, have to submit English proficiency certificates within 2 months.

所有員工，新舊皆然，都要於兩個月內交英語程度檢定證書。

※ but 但是

Monica is old but fit.
莫妮卡雖然年紀大但很健康。

They are not rich, but they always share things with others.
他們並不富有，但是總會與別人分享。

※ or 或

For this cooking competition, you can prepare within half an hour a western dish or an Asian one.
在這個烹飪比賽，你在半小時內，可以準備一道西式菜餚或一道亞洲菜。

In the end of the semester, students can choose to do a presentation or to write a paper.
在學期結束後，學生可以選擇做簡報或寫一篇論文。

Employees can apply for overtime pay, or they can take make-up leave.
員工可以申請加班費或補休。

※ yet 儘管，然而

simple yet effective
簡單但有效的

His wife is always nagging, yet somehow, he does not complain about it.

他太太總愛嘮叨，儘管如此他從未抱怨過。

※ for 因為，相當於because, as。

They had to go back without reaching the top of the mountain, for they had run out of food.
他們必須折返，無法攻頂，因為他們的食糧已經吃完了。

Andrew always wrote an e-mail to his high school teacher at Christmas, for the teacher helped him out when his family had financial problems.
安德魯總會在聖誕節時寫封電子郵件給他的高中老師，因為這位老師在他家經濟有困難時幫助了他。

※ so (that) 所以，因此

The employee worked very hard, so (that) he could get a raise.
這名員工為了能獲得加薪，非常努力工作。

Jim studies hard, so (that) he may pass the exams to be a pharmacist.
吉姆為了通過考試成為藥師，非常用功讀書。
片語對等連接詞：

both... and ... ; not ... but ... ; not only ... but　(also) ... ; either ... or ... ; neither ... nor ...
原則：句中的動詞要與最靠近的名詞一致

※ both... and...　和

Both Harry and Sally are single at that time.
哈利和莎莉那時都單身。

This chef can both cook authentic Italian cuisine and bake cake and biscuits in Italian style.
這位主廚能夠做正統的義大利料理，也能烘焙義大利風格的蛋糕和餅乾。

※ not ... but ...　並非⋯⋯而是⋯⋯

He is not a salesman but an entrepreneur.
與其說他是個業務專員，不如說他是位創業家。

Winnie is not an administrator but a coordinator.
與其說維妮是個行政人員，不如說她是協調專員。

※ not only ... but (also) ...　不但⋯⋯而且⋯⋯

To me, she is not only a good teacher but (also) a nice friend.
對我而言，她不但是良師而且也是益友。

Anthony is not only the owner of this bed & breakfast but also the tour guide and the minibus driver.
安東尼不但是這間民宿的主人，同時也是導遊兼迷你小巴駕駛。

※ either ... or ...　或（二擇一）

You can bring either a dish or beverage to the picnic.
你可以帶一道餐點或飲料來野餐。

To apply for this master program, the students have to either have done internship for at least 6 months or have won major awards in related fields.
要申請這個碩士學程，學生必須要具有六個月實習經驗，或是於相關領域中得到過大獎。

※ neither ... nor ...　既不……也不……

We should neither forget nor repeat this lesson.
我們不能忘記或是重覆這個教訓。

2. 從屬連接詞：

　　從屬連接詞所引導的子句為從屬子句，而無從屬連接詞引導的子句為主要子句，藉此表達出目的或因果的邏輯。

　　although & though & even though / in spite of & despite雖然

　　表示雖然有某種條件存在，但是還是發生了這樣的結果，例如：

Although he had much work to do, he did not complain about it.

(= He had much work to do, but he did not complain about it.)

雖然他有很多的工作要做，但是他沒有抱怨。

（於此中文翻譯當中可見，「雖然」與「但是」經常連在一起用，不過在英文，"although"與"but"不會用於同一個句子，只能擇一來使用。）

上句也可用"in spite of (despite)"表達：

In spite of (Despite) much work to do, he did not complain about it.

注意：in spite of 與despite 後要加名詞（代名詞）或動名詞。

例如：

例 In spite of the heavy workload, he is very polite to all customers.

Despite the heavy workload, he is very polite to all customers.

雖然工作量大，他還是對所有客人很有禮貌。

例 He looks all right in spite of the fact (that) he just lost his job.

He looks all right despite the fact (that) he just lost his job.

即使他剛丟了工作，他看起來好好的。

有時會用though來代替although，在口語中常常放在句末。

例如：

例 We could not go to Spain this summer though we had enough money.
雖然我們有足夠的錢，但是今年夏天我們還是不能去西班牙。

上句也可以這樣表達：

We could not go to Spain this summer. We had enough money though.
　　"Even though" 則比 "although" 又更加強語氣。

Even though we had saved up for the trip to Spain for a long time, we could not go there at the last minute.
即使我們為了去西班牙存錢存了很久，但是最後一刻我們還是不能成行。

◆ **in case**
　　由in case 所引導的子句表示「以防萬一」，例如：

例 You should take an umbrella in case it rains.
你應該帶把傘以防萬一下雨。

　　請注意in case後面用現在式來代替未來式，it rains，而非it will rain。

　　過去的時態也可以使用in case，例如：

例 Yesterday I got up one hour earlier than usual to get to school in case there was a traffic jam.
昨天我比平常還早起一個小時，以免萬一被困在堵塞的交通中。

※ unless / as long as / provided & providing

unless 表示「除非」，例句：

例 You cannot go in the basketball game unless you have a ticket.

= You cannot go in the basketball game except if you have a ticket.

= You cannot go in the basketball game only if you have a ticket.

意思等同於：If you don't have a ticket, you cannot go in the basketball game.

上面的句子意思皆相同：除非你有票，否則不能進入棒球賽場。

as long as & so long as 與 provided (that) & providing (that) 都表示條件，等同於 "if "或 "on condition that"。

例句：

例 You can borrow my book as long as you return it by the end of this month.
要是你在月底會還書才能向我借書。

請注意從屬子句中要用現在式來代替未來式，例如：

例 I can lend money to you as long as you return it tomorrow.
要是你明天還我錢，我就可以借錢給你。

◆ as
當兩件事同時發生，我們可以用 "as" 來連接這兩個子句，例句：

例 Kevin slipped as he was looking at his smartphone.
凱文在看手機時滑倒了。

例 Just as I went out, it started to rain.
我才剛出門就開始下雨了。

"as" 作為從屬連接詞還有 "because" 與 "since" 的意思

例 The host introduced him to me as I had never met him before.

= The host introduced him to me because / since I had never met him before.
因為我不曾見過他，主人介紹他給我認識。

例 You should work harder than before as your supervisor is not satisfied with your performance.

= You should work harder than before because / since your supervisor is not satisfied with your performance
你要比從前更努力工作因為你的主管對你的表現不滿意。

◆ **like & as**

like當作介系詞，後面要接名詞（代名詞）或動名詞，意思是「如同、就像」的意思。不可以用 "as" 來替代。

例如：

例 The place where you live is like an office.
你住的地方像個辦公室。

例 I like gentle sport, like swimming. (= such as)
我喜歡溫和的運動，例如游泳。

as 作為從屬連接詞有「以此方式」的意思。例如：

例 You should tidy up this room as I showed you.

= You should tidy up this room like I showed you.
（口語中可以用like代替as。）

你應該用我示範給你的方式來整理這房間。

as 作關係代名詞，有「如同」的意思，常見於下面的例子當中：

as you like / as you promise / as you know / as I said / as he thought / as they expected, etc.

As you know, the deadline of this project is coming. (=You know this already)

如同你所知的，這個專案的截止日期快要到了。

As we expected, he spent all the money he had. (= We expected this before)

如同我們預料的，他花光了所有的錢。

◆ **as if / as though**

　如果要表示「好似」，則可以用 "as if" 或 "as thou-gh"，因為與事實相反，後面要接假設法，例如：

He acts as if he knew her. （與現在事實相反）

他表現出他認識她的樣子。

He acted as though he had known her.（與過去事實相反）

那時他表現出他認識她的樣子。

　與現在事實相反的 "as if"，"as though" 後用 "were" 或 "was" 來代替 be 動詞。

例如：

例 Why do you talk about him as if he were (was) dead?

為什麼你把他當作過世的人來討論呢？

◆ **while**

　while 是用來連接同時發生的動作，例如：

例 We found many lovely shops while we were taking a walk.

我們在散步時發現了許多家可愛的店家。

例 The band members were playing music while the guests were starting to sing.

樂團演奏音樂時，客人唱起歌來。

　　如果while 後面接的是未來時態則必須用現在式代替未來式，例如：

例 What will you do while you take a year off from college studies?
你休學一年要做什麼？

例 While you stay in the city, Jessica will drop by at your hotel.
你待在這個城市時，潔西卡會順道到妳飯店拜訪妳。

牛刀小試
►TEST

1. Both Kevin _____ John are my colleagues in the law firm.

(A) with   (B) or

(C) and   (D) along

詳解

固定用法both A and B 是表示兩者皆是的意思，要注意的是A與B必須是對等的詞性。

翻譯

凱文和約翰都是我律師事務所的同事。

(C) 兩者皆

2. Not only you _____ also James has made huge progress in English during this intensive training.

(A) and   (B) but

(C) with   (D) together

詳解

固定用法not only A but also B 是表示除了A，還有B，要注意的是A與B必須是對等的詞性。

翻譯

不只是你，連建明也在這個密集訓練中進步良多。

(B) 還有

3. _____ you cannot see obvious improvement at this moment, you should keep working on the project.

(A) Although   (B) When

(C) So   (D) That

詳解

這裡需要一個連接詞來連接兩個句子，表示「雖然」的意思，所以要用although。

翻譯

即使目前你無法看見明顯的進步，你仍然要繼續努力做這個專案。

(A) 即使

4. Larry has already made several good friends _____ he moved to this area about three months ago.

(A) that   (B) if

(C) so   (D) since

詳解

完成式常要接著since來表示「自從」某個時間點之後，有一段時間都在做什麼。

翻譯

　　自從賴瑞約三個月前搬到那裡後，他結識了幾個好朋友。

　　(D) 自從

5. They stopped talking about the subject _____ they saw the boss came in with his secretary.

(A) as long as　　　　(B) as soon as

(C) as often as　　　　(D) as loud as

詳解

　　這裡要用as soon as來表示當下馬上的動作。as long as是只要的意思，as often as一樣經常，as loud as 一樣大聲。

翻譯

　　他們一看見老闆和他的秘書走進來，就馬上停止討論這個主題。

　　(B) 一……就馬上

6. The contract will go on automatically _____ you come to the office in person to cancel it.

(A) unless　　　　(B) when

(C) because　　　　(D) once

詳解

根據句意，這裡需要一個表示「除非」的連接詞，只有unless 適用。其它選項也是連接詞，意思分別為：when當，because 因為，once一旦。

翻譯

除非你本人進辦公室來終止合約，這個合約會自動繼續生效。

(A) 除非

---

7. **From now on, all staff members in this office have to work from home _____ you like it or not.**

(A) however　　　　(B) whenever

(C) whether　　　　(D) whatever

詳解

根據句意，需要的是「無論如何」的意思，只有whether… or not可以適用。其它選項分別為：wherever 無論何地，whenever無論何時，whatever無論什麼。

翻譯

從現在開始，所有員工都要遠距工作，不管你喜歡與否。

(C) 無論如何

8. _____ the law of relief funds is passed, almost all businesses can benefit much from the government aids.

(A) While   (B) Once

(C) Whereas   (D) Although

詳解

連接這兩個子句的正確連接詞，必須要有「一旦」的意思，選項中只有once符合。而其它選項也都是連接詞，意思分別是：while 當，whereas 然而，although 雖然。

翻譯

只要紓困方案通過了，幾乎所有公司都可以獲得政府補助。

(B) 只要

9. We cannot hire you _____ you provide a high TOEIC score.

(A) when   (B) unless

(C) but   (D) as

詳解

開首的子句含有否定子眼cannot（不能），所以後面要接unless（除非），以符合整句話的意思。

翻譯

除非你提供多益高分證明，我們無法雇用你。

(B) 除非

10. **Even _____ the boss raises the salary quite a lot, she still cannot find a suitable person for the position.**

    (A) when   (B) since

    (C) whereas   (D) though

詳解

這裡需要用even though這個連接詞來表示「即使」有下列狀況的意思。

翻譯

即使老闆將薪資大幅提高，仍然無法找到適合這個職缺的人。

(D) 即使

Unit 8 不定詞 & 動名詞

●不定詞

一、不定詞的用法

1. 不定詞作名詞的用法

To get up early is impossible to me.
早起對我來說不可能。

2. 不定詞作形容詞的用法

You need a job to make a living.
你需要份工作來維生。

3. 不定詞作副詞的用法

She was trained to be an English teacher.
她受過作為英文老師的訓練。

※ 不定詞的否定式：於不定詞前加上 not

My mother told me not to go out too late.
我母親要我不要太晚出門。

二、不定詞原形的用法

※ 省略to的情況

1. 於感官動詞（see, watch, hear）後面出現的不定詞

I saw her walk out of the room.
我看見她走出房間。

2. 於使役動詞（make, have, let）後面出現的不定詞

The nurse made her take the medicine.
護理師要她服用藥物。

以上感官動詞與使役動詞改用被動時，to 不能省略。

She was seen to walk out of the room.
她被人看見走出房間。

三、不定詞的時態

1. 時間與動詞時態一致

He seemed to be very angry.
他似乎很生氣。

2. 時間較動詞時態早

He seemed to have been angry.
他似乎很生氣過。

3. 不定詞放於hope, want 後，表示未來

He wants to see her again.
他希望能再見她一面。

4. 不定詞的常用片語

※ too... to...　太……而不能……

She is too old to work.
她年紀太大而不能工作。

※ so... that... = so... as to... = so... enough to...
如此……以至於……

He is so poor that he has to sell his house.

= He is so poor as to sell his house.
他如此窮以至於要賣房子。

He is so smart that he can understand it.

= He is smart enough to understand it.
他是如此聰明以至於他能理解這件事。

●動名詞

一、動名詞的用法

1. 當主詞

Speaking in public is not easy.
公眾演講不容易。

2. 當受詞

I do not like speaking in public.
我不喜歡在公眾場合演講。

3. 當受詞補語

We call Mr.Chen "a Walking Dictionary".
我們稱陳先生為"會走路的字典"。

二、動名詞的時態

1. 表示與動詞相同或之後的時間

※ 相同的時間

She is interested in singing.
她對歌唱感興趣。

※ 之後的時間

She is interested in becoming a singer after graduation.
她想要於畢業後當歌星。

(2) 表示比動詞更早的時間

She is proud of having been a singer.
她對於從前當過歌星感到驕傲。

3. 動名詞的常用片語

※ It/There is no use ~ ing ……沒有用

There is no use crying over spilt milk.
覆水難收。

It is no use regretting it.
後悔沒有用。

※ feel like ~ ing 想要……

I feel like crying.
我感到想哭。

They feel like breaking down.
他們感到快崩潰。

※ cannot help ~ ing 忍不住……

They couldn't help crying upon hearing the news.
他們聽到消息後忍不住哭起來。

※ be busy ~ ing 忙著……

Recently I have been busy learning Japanese.
最近我忙著學日語。

三、動名詞與不定詞的比較

1. 後面接動名詞與不定詞都可以的動詞：

◆ **begin, start, like, love...**

例句：

例 When did you begin to work?
= When did you begin working?
你什麼時候開始工作？

例 Laura likes to sing.

= Laura likes singing.
蘿拉喜歡唱歌。

2. 只能由動名詞當受詞的動詞：

◆ **enjoy, finish, mind...**

例句：

例 Larry enjoys interviewing people.
賴瑞喜愛訪問人。

例 When will you finish writing the book?
你什麼時候會寫完這本書？

例 Would you mind opening the window for me?
你介意幫我打開窗戶嗎？

3. 只能由不定詞當受詞的動詞：

◆ **want, wish, hope, decide...**

例句：

例 Most children want to go to an amusement park.
大部分小孩子想要去遊樂園。

例 Finally, I decided to tell her the truth.
最後我決定告訴她實情。

---

4. 由動名詞與由不定詞當受詞意思不同的動詞：

---

forget, remember, stop, go on, regret, try, mean, need...

※ forget 忘記

forget 後接不定詞，表示忘記要做某件事。

例 Don't forget to turn off the heater before you leave the room.

例 = Don't forget you have to turn off the heater before you leave the room.
離開房間前不要忘記關暖器。

forget 後接動名詞，表示已經做了某件事。

Jane forgot feeding the dog.

= Jane forgot that she had fed the dog.
珍忘記已經餵過狗。

※ remember 記得

remember 後接不定詞，表示記得要去做某件事。

I still remember to do the laundry.
我記得要去洗衣服。

remember 後接動名詞，表示記得做過某件事。

I remember doing the laundry.
我記得已經洗過衣服。

※ stop 停止

stop 後接不定詞，表示停下來要去做某件事。

Jennifer stopped to send the card.
珍妮佛停下來去寄卡片。

stop 後接動名詞，表示停止做某件事。

Jennifer stopped sending cards after e-mail was invented.
珍妮佛於電子郵件發明後就停止了寄卡片。

※ go on 繼續

go on 後接不定詞，表示接下來要去做某件事。

The professor went on to tell us about the assignment.
教授停下來告訴我們有關作業的事。

go on 後接動名詞，表示繼續做某件事。

The professor went on telling us about the assignment.
教授不停地告訴我們有關作業的事。

※ regret 後悔

regret 後接不定詞，表示很遺憾接下來要做某件事。

I regret to tell you that I am not going to work here anymore.
很遺憾地我必須告訴你，我將不再於這裡工作。

regret 後接動名詞，表示後悔做了某件事。

He regretted telling her his secret.
他後悔告訴她他的秘密。

※ try 嘗試

try 後接不定詞，表示嘗試去做某件事。

Have you tried to tell him this?
你嘗試告訴過他嗎？

try 後接動名詞，表示試試看做某件事，比起try 後接不定詞來說較不費力。

Why don't you try writing down your thoughts?
為什麼你不試著寫下你的感覺呢？

※ mean

mean 後接不定詞，表示意圖去做某件事，意同於intend。

She meant to fire me.
她意圖要開除我。

mean 後接動名詞，表示「意即為、意味著」，意同於「涉及」（involve）。

Moving out of parents' places means having to pay all living costs by oneself.
搬離父母的家意味著要自己負擔所有的生活費用。

※ need

人+ need + 不定式：表示「需要」。

She needed to take a rest.
她需要休息一下。

※ 物 + need + 動名詞：含有被動含意。

意即為：

物 + need + 被動不定式：含有被動含意。

The carpet needs cleaning.
地毯需要清理。

意即為：

The carpet needs to be cleaned.
地毯需要清理。

►TEST

1. Lucy hates _____ a chubby girl.

(A) to be calling   (B) called

(C) be called   (D) being called

詳解

　　這裡需要使用動名詞來表示討厭某事，而討厭「被叫作胖妹」是被動的，所以要用being called。

翻譯

　　露西討厭被叫作胖妹。

(D) 被叫作

2. It hurt so much that I could not help _____.

(A) cry   (B) cryed

(C) to cry   (D) crying

詳解

　　這裡常用片語cannot help 表示「忍不住」的意思，後面固定要加上動名詞。

翻譯

　　我痛到忍不住哭了出來。

(D) cry的動名詞crying。

3. Please remember _____ the postcard on your way to the office.

(A) sending   (B) to send

(C) have sent   (D) having sent

詳解

remember後面可以接不定詞也可接動名詞，但意思不一樣：接不定詞，表示記得要去做某件未做之事，而接動名詞則表示記得做過某件事。

翻譯

上班途中，請記得寄這張明信片。

(B) send的不定詞to send。

4. Jack has trouble _____ with his English teacher.

(A) communicates   (B) communicate

(C) communicating   (D) to communicate

詳解

常用片語have trouble後面固定要加上動名詞，表示在某方面有困難。

翻譯

傑克跟英語老師溝通有困難。

(C) communicate的動名詞 communicating。

5. **What would you want _____ when you grow up?**

(A) do   (B) to do

(C) have done   (D) doing

詳解

因為意思是未來想要做什麼，所以要用不定詞。

翻譯

你長大後想要做什麼？

(B) do的不定詞to do。

6. **Would you mind _____ here?**

(A) to smoke   (B) my smoking

(C) mine smoking   (D) smoke

詳解

問對方是否介意的常用片語為Would you mind⋯ 後面固定要接動名詞，所以要接my smoking。

翻譯

您介意我於此抽菸嗎？

(B) 我抽菸

7. He forgot _____ the old man several days ago.

(A) seen   (B) to see

(C) has seen   (D) having seen

詳解

　　forget後面可以接不定詞也可接動名詞，但意思不一樣：接不定詞，表示忘記要去做某事，而接動名詞則表示忘記做了某件事，而在這裡指的是已經見過某人，所以要用完成式的動名詞having seen。

翻譯

　　他忘了幾天前見過這個老人。

　　(D) 曾經見過。

8. This scenic spot is very worth _____.

(A) visit   (B) visiting

(C) to visit   (D) visited

詳解

　　「值得」常用片語be worth，後面固定接動名詞，worth visiting值得一遊, worth seeing值得一見, worth reading值得一讀。

翻譯

　　這個景點很值得一遊。

(B) visit的動名詞visiting。

9. She stopped _____ with her ex-husband as soon as he got married again because she did not want to upset his second wife.

(A) talked   (B) talking

(C) to talk   (D) talk

詳解

　　stop 後面可以接不定詞也可接動名詞，但意思不一樣：接不定詞，表示停下來去做某事，而接動名詞則表示停止做某件正在進行的事。在這裡根據句意應該要接動名詞，表示停止再跟前夫談話。

翻譯

　　她前夫再婚後她就馬上停止跟前夫談話，因為不想要讓他第二任妻子不開心。

　　(B) talking: 亦即是talk的動名詞。

10. Don't forget _____ off the light when you go out.

(A) turn   (B) to turn

(C) turning   (D) turned

詳解

　　forget後面可以接不定詞也可接動名詞，但意思不一樣：接不定詞，表示忘了去做某事，而接動名詞則表示

忘記做了某件事，這裡是在提醒人不要忘了要做什麼事，
所以要用不定詞to turn。

翻譯

離開時別忘了關燈。

(B) turn的不定詞to turn。

Unit 9 助動詞

● 一、助動詞的定義

助動詞本身並沒有詞義，它是用來幫助主要動詞（Main Verb）形成各種時態、語氣、語態、疑問句、或否定句。最常使用的助動詞有：do (do, does, did) 、have (have, has, had) 、be (am, are, is, was, were, be, being, been) 、will, shall, can, may (would, should, could, might) 等等。

● 二、助動詞的分類

助動詞的種類：

1. 一般助動詞：do, have, be, will

用來形成：(1) 疑問句 (2) 附加問句 (3) 否定句 (4) 加強語氣

(1) do

第三人稱單數：does

過去式：did

◆ 疑問句

Do you review the lessons every day?
你是否每天複習功課？

◆ 否定句

He does not believe in God.
他不相信上帝。

◆ 過去式

At that time, most schools did not have facilities for the people with disabilities.
在那個時候，大部分學校沒有身心障礙設施。
簡單現在式的強調

They do work hard for the future.
為了未來他們真的很拼。

◆ 簡單過去式的強調

The students did try their best to save up for their school outing this summer.
這些學生為了夏季校外教學真的很盡力存錢。

---

(2) have

與過去分詞一起構成各種完成式。

第三人稱單數：has

過去式：had

◆ 疑問句

Have you ever been to Europe?
你曾經去過歐洲嗎？

◆ 否定句

We have never seen such a brilliant student.
我們從來沒見過這樣聰明的學生。

◆ 過去完成式

His mother told the teacher that he had been terribly ill.
他的母親告訴老師他有一陣子得了重病。

◆ 現在完成進行式

He has been lying to his teacher since the beginning.
他一開始就對老師撒謊。

◆ 分詞完成式

Having told one lie, he has to make up another one.
說了一個謊之後，他只得再撒一個謊。

---

(3) be

與現在分詞一起構成各種進行式

與過去分詞一起構成被動式

am/is/are

was/were

being

been

◆ 現在進行式

The substitute teacher is writing the topic of English composition on the blackboard.
代課老師在黑板上寫下英文作文的題目。

◆ 過去進行式

We were making progress in English.
我們英文進步很多。

◆ 簡單現在被動式

Nobody likes to be scolded.
沒有人喜歡挨罵。

---

(4) will

與動詞原形一起構成未來式

現在式：will

過去式：would

◆ 簡單未來式

Quite a few people believe that she will win the champion.
非常多人認為她會贏得冠軍。

◆ 過去未來式

Contrary to what we expected, Linda would not work for her company anymore.
出乎我們意料之外，琳達不會再為她公司工作。

2. 情態助動詞

(1) can

※ **表示能力** = be able to

Can you speak English?
你會說英語嗎？

We can demonstrate it for you.
我們能為您示範。

※ **表示准許**

Nobody can see him without making an appointment.
沒有人能不預約就與他會面。

Can I smoke here?
我可以在這裡抽菸嗎？

※ **表示可能性**

I don't know who has been here. Can it be your landlord?
我不清楚誰到過這裡，會是你的房東嗎？

※ **表示請求（常與 please 連用）**

Can you please stop making noise?
你可以停止製造噪音嗎？

(2) could

※ 是can 的過去式

We could not afford many items back then.
我們那時無法負擔很多事物。

※ 表示過去的能力

Misha could speak a bit Russian in high school.
米夏在高中時會說一點俄語。

※ 表示容許，比could 委婉

Could you please stop smoking?
你可以戒菸嗎？

(3) may

※ 表示准許

May I leave classroom and go home?
我可以離開教室回家嗎？

※ 表示可能性

This typhoon may come or may not come.
這個颱風可能會來也可能不會來。

※ 表示祈願

May all your wishes come true!
但願你的願望都能成真！

※ 與not 連用，表示禁止

You may not take the items here away.
你不能拿走這裡的東西。

(4) might

※ 是may 的過去式

This might not be a good idea.
這或許不是個好點子。

※ 表示比may 更小的可能性

We might not be able to find this parcel ever again.
我們可能無法再找到這個包裹。

(5) will

※ 表示單純未來

It seems we will finish this project in time.
看來我們似乎可以及時完成這個專案。

It will rain tomorrow.
明天會下雨。

※ 表示意願、承諾

Will you marry me?
你願意嫁給（娶）我嗎？

※ 表示請求

Will you please turn down the volume a bit?
可以請你將音量調低一點嗎？

※ 表示主張、決心

I will never trust any man again.
我不會再相信任何男人。

※ 表示習慣

We will eat desserts after dinners.
我們是在晚飯後吃甜點的。

(6) would

※ 是 will 的過去式

Rita would go mountain climbing when she had time off in high school.
麗塔高中放假時會去爬山。

※ 表示比 will 更委婉的請求，常用於問句

Would you please quit smoking?
請你戒菸好嗎？

※ 表示過去的習慣

At that time, he would smoke a cigarette after meals.
他那時會在飯後抽一根菸。

※ 表示意願，常與 like, love 連用

I would like to teach children English.
我想要教小孩英語。

※ would rather （常與 than 連用）

◆ 表示比較喜歡

I would rather go in nature than stay home.
比起待在家裡，我比較喜歡去大自然走走。

◆ 否定式，用 **would rather not**

She would rather not return to her home country.
她寧願不回她自己的國家。

(7) must

※ 表示義務

Almost all young men in this country must do military service.
在這個國家幾乎所有年輕男生都要服兵役。

※ 表示必然

It must be you.
一定是你。

※ 表示重要性

One must lock the door before leaving this place.
離開這裡前一定要鎖門。

※ 過去式時要用 had to

She had to call her husband because she needed his computer.
她必須要打電話給她先生，因為她必須要用他的電腦。

※ 與 not 連用表示禁止

You must not complain to your boss.
你不該向你的老闆抱怨。

(8) need

※ 當助動詞時，用於否定句及疑問句

You needn't worry too much for your child.
你不需要為你小孩太過擔心。

Need we bring some food to your place?
我們需要帶什麼食物到你家嗎？

※ 當主要動詞時，變化如同一般動詞

Maybe we don't need to do anything.
或許我們不需要做任何事。

(9) shall

※ 常用於第一人稱的問句

Shall we go?
我們該走了嗎？

Shall I make tea for you?
需要我為你泡杯茶嗎？

※ 用於第一人稱，表示決心

I shall come back.
我會回來的。

※ 用於第二或第三人稱，表示絕對與義務

You shall come here on time tomorrow morning.
你明早要準時到這裡。

※ 用於附加問句表示邀請

Let's go to the movie, shall we?
我們一起去看電影好嗎？

(10) should

※ 是 shall 的過去式

Lisa should be able to provide you with the information you need.
麗莎會提供你所需要的資訊給你。

※ 表示義務，等於 ought to

We should not forget the lesson of WWII.
我們不該忘記第二次世界大戰的教訓。

※ 與 why 連用於問句中，表示驚奇

Why should we do so much for our children?
我們為何要替小孩做這麼多事？

(11) ought to

※ 表示義務 = should

People ought to care for the aged.
人們應該照顧長者。

※ 表示建議

We ought to tell him about this.
我們應該告訴他相關事項。

※ 表示期待

They are unsure what they ought to do.
他們不確定該做什麼事。

※ 否定式

People ought not to take everything for granted.
人們不該將所有事視為理所當然。

※ 疑問句

Ought she to see a dentist?
她該去看牙醫嗎？

(12) used to

※ 表示過去的習慣

When Tim was working, he used to get up very early to learn English.
提姆還在工作時，他總是每天很早起床來學習英語。

※ 否定式used not to

Jerry used not to talk to so many people in English.
傑瑞那時不習慣在這麼多人面前說英語。

比較片語：be/get used to ＋ N / V-ing 習慣於

（此處的to為介系詞，後面要加名詞或動名詞）

例句：

例 He is used to working so many hours a week.
他習慣一星期工作這麼多時數。

例 She got used to getting up in the early morning.
她習慣每天早起。

1. All workers in the company _____ wear uni forms. It is stated in the company's Code of Conduct.

(A) can   (B) must

(C) may   (D) have

詳解

在這裡需要用一個表示義務的主動詞，所有選項中只有must意思是「該做的」。

翻譯

所有公司員工都必須要穿制服，員工守則中有規定。

(B) must 必須

2. This document _____ have been produced by him. He does not even know how to use a computer.

(A) needn't   (B) should

(C) must   (D) can't

詳解

這裡需要表示不可能的推測，所以要使用can't。

翻譯

這份文件不可能是他製作的，他連電腦都不會使用。

(D) can't 不可能是。

3. You _____ bought that fax machine in October because there is now an end-of-year sale in the shop.

(A) shouldn't have   (B) couldn't have

(C) wouldn't have   (D) cannot have

詳解

這裡的句意是說十月時不該買傳真機，因為大可以等到現在店家年終大拍賣再買，後悔已經做了的事，要用shouldn't have加上過去分詞。

翻譯

你十月時不該買傳真機，因為現在店家在年終大拍賣。

(A) shouldn't have 不該

4. There _____ some rumors about her pregnancy.

(A) used to have   (B) used to be

(C) used to having   (D) used to being

詳解

意思是當時有些傳聞，there is中間加上助動詞used to於是成了 there used to be。

翻譯

當時有些關於她懷孕的傳聞。

(B) used to be 當時有。

5. You _____ study hard if you want to pass the final exam.

(A) will

(B) could

(C) should

(D) might

詳解

表示必須做某件事，要用助動詞should。

翻譯

你必須要努力唸書才能通過期末考。

(C) should 必須

6. If you _____ have doubt about his identity, look it up in the Internet.

(A) could

(B) would

(C) will

(D) should

詳解

助動詞should在這裡表示要是萬一的意思。

翻譯

萬一你懷疑他的身分，在網路上查一下。

(D) should 萬一

7. You _____ have the book if you like it.

(A) can　　　　　　(B) will

(C) shall　　　　　(D) need

詳解

這裡只有can能夠表示「可以」的意思。

翻譯

要是你喜歡，這本書可以給你。

(A) can 可以

8. Who _____ possibly made up such a story and spread around the social media?

(A) will　　　　　(B) shall

(C) could　　　　(D) may

詳解

這裡只有could能夠表示「推測可能性」的意思。

翻譯

有誰會杜撰這樣的故事，然後在社群媒體上散播呢？

(C) could 會

9. You cannot really mean it, _____ you?

(A) don't   (B) can

(C) will   (D) won't

詳解

附加問句只要用同樣的助動詞即可，通常前面用肯定，附加問句則用否定；前面用否定，附加問句則用肯定。

翻譯

你該不會是當真的吧？

(B) can

10. Let's go shopping, _____ we?

(A) do   (B) shall

(C) have   (D) might

詳解

表示邀請的句子Let's…. 附加問句常用shall we。

翻譯

我們一起去購物吧！

(B) shall

Unit 10 假設法

● 一、假設法的種類

1. 與現在事實相反

If + 主詞 + 動詞過去式 , 主詞 + would (should, might, could) + 動詞原形

If I were you, I might take sick leave.
要是我是你,我可能會請病假。

If Leo could control his temper, he would be a successful businessman.
要是利歐能控制他的脾氣,他可能會是個成功的企業家。

2. 與過去事實相反

If + 主詞 + had + 過去分詞 , 主詞 + would + have + 過去分詞

If I had known it, I would have told you.
我那時要是知道的話,我就會告訴你。

If Stacy had saved money, she could have afforded a trip to Paris.
要是史黛西之前有存錢的話,她可能就能負擔得起

巴黎之旅。

◎ If ＋ 與過去事實相反，主要子句：與現在事實相反

If ＋ 主詞 ＋ had ＋ 過去分詞，主詞 ＋ would (should, might, could) ＋ 動詞原形

If I had taken up the position, I would be the manager of the company now.
要是那時我接受這個職位，現在我或許就是這家公司的經理。

If I had worked harder, I could be on vacation right now.
要是那時我更努力工作，現在我可能就在渡假了。

3. 表達未來萬一的情形

If ＋ 主詞 ＋ should ＋ 動詞原形，主詞 ＋ will, shall, can, may ＋ 動詞原形

If I should win the lottery, I shall purchase a mansion with a garden.
要是我中了樂透，我就要買一棟附有花園的豪宅。

● 二、假設法的特殊用法

1. I wish

I wish I were a successful entrepreneur.
但願我是個成功的企業家。

I wish I had been a successful entrepreneur.
但願我那時是個成功的企業家。

2. as if / as though

He acts as if / as though he didn't know me.
他表現得好像不認識我。

He acted as if / as though he had not known me.
他那時表現得好像不認識我。

3. but for/without

But for her help, I would not be working in this company now.
要不是有她的幫忙，現在我不可能有辦法在這裡工作。

Without Simon's support, I would not have made it to the end.
那時要不是有賽門的幫忙，我不可能有辦法完成工作。

4. 省略 if

省略了 if，則需要將 be 動詞 (were) , had, 助動詞 (should) 放置句首。

例一：

例 If I were you, I would quit the job.
--> 省略 if

Were I you, I would quit the job.
要是我是你，我就會辭職。

例二：

例 If I had the money, I would travel around the world.
--> 省略 if

Had I the money, I would travel around the world.
要是我有錢，我就會環遊世界。

例三：

例 If it should snow, the event will not take place.
--> 省略 if

Should it snow, the event will not take place.
萬一下雪的話，這個活動就不會舉行。

例四：

例 If I had had the time, I would have talked to him about it.
--> 省略 if

Had I had the time, I would have talked to him about it.
要是那時我有時間的話，我會跟他談這件事。

牛刀小試
►TEST

1. If I _____ you, I would be contented.

(A) be   (B) am

(C) were   (D) are

詳解

與現在事實相反的be動詞要用were。

翻譯

如果我是你，我會知足。

(C) were與現在事實相反。

2. _____ I you, I would tell the truth now.

(A) Be   (B) Am

(C) Were   (D) Are

詳解

假設法若要用倒裝來強調，只需要將were放在句首即可。

翻譯

如果我是你，我會說實話。

(C) Were

3. _____ you written him an e-mail to inform him, he would have attended the workshop.

(A) Should   (B) If

(C) Have   (D) Had

詳解

這裡是過去假設法的倒裝，只需要將助動詞had放在句首即可。

翻譯

要是當時你寫了封電子郵件告知他，他就會參加這個工作坊。

(D) Had

4. If you _____ told the truth, you wouldn't be in such a big trouble.

(A) have had   (B) had

(C) have   (D) did

詳解

與過去事實相反，所以要用had加上過去分詞，要注意的是後面是與現在事實相反。

翻譯

要是你當時說實話，現在就不會惹這麼大的麻煩。

(B) had

5. _____ you applied two week earlier, you would have been accepted.

(A) Have   (B) Had

(C) If   (D) When

詳解

　　這是與過去事實相反的假設法加上倒裝，所以只要將助動詞had放在句首即可。

翻譯

　　要是你早兩個星期申請，你就會被錄取。

(B) Had

6. If you had told me that your mother was ill, I _____ have let you work from home.

(A) will   (B) won't

(C) would   (D) wouldn't

詳解

　　與過去事實相反的假設，根據句意應該用would have let。

翻譯

　　要是當時你告訴了我你母親生病，我會讓你在家工作。

(C) would

7. I strongly suggest you _____ study our company's rules on leave-taking much more carefully.

(A) can　　　　　(B) should

(C) shall　　　　(D) might

詳解

因為strongly suggest強烈建議，所以後面要用should來表示該做的動作。

翻譯

我強烈建議你更仔細研讀公司請假規定。

(B) should

8. I wish I _____ a bird!

(A) am　　　　　(B) be

(C) were　　　　(D) to be

詳解

I wish（但願）後面接的陳述與現在事實相反，所以要用were。

翻譯

但願我是隻小鳥。

(C) were

9. The judge ordered the case _____ dismissed.

(A) be   (B) is

(C) been   (D) to be

詳解

因為動詞order所以後面要接should加上原形動詞，而should可省略，所以才會出現be在單數名詞後。

翻譯

此案被法官駁回。

(A) be

10. If we _____ the problem, we would have done all we could to prevent it from happening.

(A) known   (B) have known

(C) knew   (D) had known

詳解

典型與過去事實相反的假設法，所以要使用had known。

翻譯

要是那時我們知道這個問題，我們就會盡全力去避免這事發生。

(D) had known

Unit 11 關係詞

● 一、關係代名詞 (Relative Pronouns)

關係代名詞兼具代名詞與連接詞兩種角色，一方面代替前面的先行詞（名詞或代名詞），另一方面則引導關係子句來修飾所替代的先行詞。

1. 關係代名詞的種類：who, whom, whose, which, that, as, than, what。

◎ who

who 為人的關係代名詞。

Do you know the tall girl who is standing over there?
你認識站在那邊的高個子女孩嗎？

◎ whom

關係代名詞 whom 為 who 的受格，口語中可以用 who 代替，也可以省略。

You should not trust someone whom you just met.
你不應該信賴剛剛才認識的人。

◎ whose

為who 的所有格。

There came the guest whose name I happen to forget.
迎面走來這位客人，他的名字我剛好忘了。

◎ which

which為事物的關係代名詞。

※ 限定性用法

如果關係代名詞所引導的形容詞子句具有「限制住」所修飾的先行詞為哪些的功能，稱為限定性用法，此關係代名詞之前不要加逗號。

The place which you recommended is very worth visiting.
你推薦的地方非常值得一遊。

※ 非限定性用法

如果關係代名詞所引導的形容詞子句是用來補充說明先行詞的性質，不具有「限制住」是哪些先行詞的功能，稱為非限定性用法，此關係代名詞引領的子句前後要加逗號。

The 3 books, which you picked, become the best sellers of the year.
這三本你所挑的書成為今年最佳暢銷書。

Kazuo Ishiguro, who wrote "The Remains of the Day", was the winner of the 2017 Nobel prize in literature 2017.

著有《長日將盡》的石黑一雄獲得了 2017 年的諾貝爾文學獎。

◎ that

先行詞為人或事物，前面的修飾語為：形容詞最高級, all, every, any, the same, the only, the very等等。

The tallest boy that you see there is my son.
那邊你所看到最高的男孩是我的兒子。

All that glitters is not gold.
閃閃發亮的並不都是金子。

The only thing that you should remember to do for me is to thank her.
你唯一該幫我做的事就是向她道謝。

◎ as

與 such, the same, as... 連用，在形容詞子句中作主詞或受詞。

Mandy is the same sweet girl as we knew in school.
曼蒂仍然是我們在學期間所認識的那個甜美的女孩。

◎ than

通常用於 "形容詞比較級 + 名詞" 之後，而比較級後面的名詞則為than 的先行詞。在這個地方，than 當作關係代名詞，than之前的名詞為先行詞，也就是比較級所修飾的名詞。

Don't let your children have more money than is needed.
不要讓你的小孩有超過需要的錢。

◎ what

what = the thing which, that which, all that, anything that

前面不會有先行詞

Don't believe what the guy told you.
不要相信這個人告訴你的。

What we see is often the reflections of our thoughts.
我們所看見的經常是我們內心想法的反映。

●二、關係副詞 (Relative Adverb)

關係副詞（where, when, why, how）通常用來取代介系詞和關係代名詞which，由關係副詞所形成的關係子句用來修飾前面的名詞。

1. 關係副詞分為 where, when, why, how。

◎ where 代替地方

the place 和 where 當中可以省略其中之一，但不能同時省略。

I have never been to the place where the film was shot.

= I have never been to where the film was shot.

= I have never been to the place the film was shot.
我從來沒去過那部電影拍攝的地點。

This is the city where he works now.

= This is the city in which he works now.
這是他現在工作所在的城市。

That is the beach where most people like to practice surfing.

= That is the beach on which most people like to practice surfing.
那就是大部分人喜歡練習衝浪的海灘。

◎ when 代替時間

the time 和 when 當中可以省略其中之一，但不能同時省略。

Do you remember the time when we met each other?

= Do you remember when we met each other?

= Do you remember the time we met each other?
你記得我們何時第一次相遇嗎？

That was the day when I first heard of his name.

= That was the day on which I first heard of his name.
那是我聽到他名字的第一天。

◎ why 代替理由

the reason 和 why 當中可以省略其中之一，但不能同時省略。

Nobody knows the reason why she fell ill.

= Nobody knows why she fell ill.

= Nobody knows the reason she fell ill.
沒有人知道她為何生病。

The reason why she dropped out was unknown.

= The reason for which she dropped out was unknown.
她輟學的原因沒有人知道。

◎ how 代替方式

Do you know how he learned Korean?
你知道他學韓語的原因嗎？

= Do you know the way he learned Korean?
你知道他學習韓語的方法嗎？

the way 與 how 不可連在一起用

現代英文文法家認為 the way 與 how 意思重複，因此只要於二者擇一來使用，不要兩者放在一起用。

2. 用法

※ 限定性用法

例句：

例 My parents run a hotel where many senior citizens spend their holidays.

我父母經營一家很多銀髮族在那兒渡假的旅館。

關係副詞對於所修飾的先行詞有限定的作用，稱為限定性用法，例如在這個例子中，特別指的是所有旅館當中，來客有很多銀髮族的旅館。

※ 非限定性用法

例句：

例 Anthony would like to spend holidays in Japan, where he can learn to ski.

安東尼想要在日本渡假，在那兒他可以學滑雪。

關係副詞對於所修飾的先行詞只有修飾作用，沒有限定的作用，稱為非限定性用法，關係副詞前要加逗號，例如此例中，日本是全世界獨一無二的，自然不用再加以限定。

1. Those _____ come too late may not get a free bobble milk tea because too many people are waiting in a line.

(A) which   (B) who

(C) whereas   (D) whose

詳解

主詞those是those people的簡寫,所以要用關係代名詞who來代替,意思是「那些」遲到的人。

翻譯

那些太晚到的人可能沒法得到免費珍珠奶茶,因為太多人在排隊。

(B) 那些人的關係代名詞

2. The students _____ parents are in a quarantine hotel should not come to school.

(A) which   (B) who

(C) whom   (D) whose

詳解

意思是指學生們的,所以要用whose所有格關係代名詞來代替「他們的」。

翻譯

那些父母親待在防疫旅館的學生，不應該來學校。

(D) 他們的所有格關係代名詞

3. **The population of Tokyo is bigger than _____ of Taipei.**

(A) what   (B) that

(C) whose   (D) who

詳解

只有相同屬性的東西才可以比較，而用來比較之物，第二次提及，如果是單數要用that來當代名詞，複數則要用those來當代名詞。

翻譯

東京的人口比台北的人口多。

(B) 比較時單數代名詞

4. **Some people might not like the painting, _____ seems to tell many unusual stories at one time.**

(A) which   (B) that

(C) where   (D) who

詳解

這裡要用物品的關係代名詞which來代替前面的painting。

翻譯

很多人可能不喜歡這幅畫，這幅畫似乎同時在訴說很多不尋常的故事。

(A) 物品的關係代名詞

5. **The singer was born in a simple farming village, _____ many indigenous families grow rice and fruit.**

(A) which (B) when

(C) where (D) that

詳解

這裡要用地方的關係代名詞where來代替前面的village。

翻譯

這位歌星出生在一個簡樸的農村，在那裡很多原住民家庭種植稻米和水果。

(C) 地方的關係代名詞

6. **Call me or drop by _____ you have come up with new ideas about how to proceed the project.**

(A) wherever (B) whoever

(C) whenever (D) whichever

詳解

　　這裡需要的是whenever來表示無論何時。其它的選項分別為wherever 無論何地，whoever 無論何人，whichever任何。

翻譯

　　你有新主意時隨時都可打電話給我或來找我。

　　(C) 無論何時，隨時

7. **Do not believe all things you hear; you have to think over ＿＿＿＿ others tell you.**

　　(A) which　　　　　(B) whenever

　　(C) whatever　　　(D) however

詳解

　　這裡要用whatever來表示任何事情。其它選項分別為which關係代名詞，前面沒有名詞所以不可用；whenever無論何時，however無論如何。

翻譯

　　不要相信你聽到的任何事，你應該要對所有事加以思考。

　　(C) 任何事

8. The old man in a wheelchair _____ you saw entering the clinic is Jenny's father-in-law.

(A) whom　　　　　(B) when

(C) what　　　　　(D) where

詳解

這裡要用人稱關係代名詞who的受格whom，也可以用who來代替。

翻譯

你看到坐在輪椅正進房間的老人，是珍妮的公公。

(A) whom是who的受詞

9. James is the best assistant _____ his boss has had so far and he is quite humble.

(A) which　　　　　(B) whom

(C) whom　　　　　(D) that

詳解

因為有形容詞最高級the best，所以關係代名詞要用that。

翻譯

建銘是他老闆至今的最佳助理，而且他相當謙虛。

(D) 形容詞最高級的關係代名詞

10. No matter _____ happens to you, you can always count on me.

    (A) what　　　　　　(B) that

    (C) whatever　　　　(D) which

詳解

　　這裡要表達的是「無論什麼事」，所以要用no matter what，也就是whatever的意思，但是不可以在no matter後再加上whatever。

翻譯

　　無論你發生什麼事都可以靠我。

　　(A) 無論

Unit 12 分詞與分詞構句

●一、分詞

現在分詞（動詞字尾加上 -ing）

表示動作為主動，正在進行中。

過去分詞（動詞字尾加上 -ed 或不規則變化）

表示動作為被動，已經完成。

分詞放於be 動詞或have 之後。

例句：

例 I am reading a book.（現在分詞）
我正在讀一本書。

例 The book is read by many people.（過去分詞）
這本書為很多人所讀。

例 We all have read the book.（過去分詞）
我們都讀過這本書。

●二、分詞構句

用分詞構成副詞性片語，不使用連接詞，若子句的
主詞與主要子句的主詞相同時，子句的主詞可以省略。
分詞構句是一種從屬副詞子句，用來修飾主要字句，形

式如下：

（從屬連接詞） ＋ V-ing / V-en, S ＋ V

例句：

例 Eating dinner, she saw interesting commercials on TV.
她一邊看吃飯一邊看有趣的電視廣告。

例 Taken with lemon juice, the honey tea tastes really good.
加上檸檬汁的蜂蜜茶真好喝。

形成的步驟如下：

(1) 先看主要子句與副詞子句的主詞是否相同。

(2) 如果主詞相同的話，可以刪除副詞子句的主詞；如果主詞不同的話，則要保留副詞子句的主詞。主要子句的主詞如果是代名詞，而副詞子句的主詞為名詞時，於刪去副詞子句的主詞時，記得要將主要子句的主詞還原為名詞。

(3) 將從屬子句中動詞前的情態助動詞或 do 刪除，然後將從屬子句的動詞改為 V-ing 或 V-en，be 動詞則為改為 being。

(4) 從屬連結接詞可視狀況刪除或保留。

(5) being V-ing, being Adj 與 being V-en 當中可以省略 being。

(6) having V-ing 可視語意改為upon V-ing, on V-ing 或 after V-ing。

●三、分詞構句的功能

分詞構句的功能如下：

◎ 時間

When he felt hungry, he went to the cafeteria.

-->Feeling hungry, he went to the cafeteria.
他覺得餓了就去自助餐廳。

◎ 原因

As he had no money, he could not buy the movie ticket.

-->Having no money, he could not buy the movie ticket.
因為沒有錢所以他無法買電影票。

Because it is read by many generations of students, the story has become a classic novel.

-->Read by many generations of students, the story has become a classic novel.
因為世世代代的學生都讀過這本書，所以這本書成了經典小說。

◎ 條件

If you go straight, you will see the bank.

-->Going straight, you will see the bank.
如果你一直向前走就會看見銀行。

◎ 讓步

Although he is poor and sick, he often helps those in need.

-->Being poor and sick, he often helps those in need.
雖然他又窮又病，他還是經常幫助需要的人。

Even though he was beaten up by the bully, he still would not give in.

-->Beaten up by the bully, he still would not give in.
雖然他被霸凌者痛打，他仍然不退讓。

可於分詞前加上not形成否定。

Not knowing what to do, he called his parents for help.
他不知道該如何是好，只好打電話給父母求救。

•四、垂懸結構（Danglers）

以帶有分詞開頭的句子

錯誤：

Seeing his mother return home, the television was turned off immediately.

一看見他母親回來，電視馬上就被關了。

正確：

Seeing his mother return home, he turned off the television immediately.

他一看見母親回來，就馬上關了電視。

慣用片語例外

這些慣用片語長久以來為人用來作為開場白習慣用語，因此不需要與主要子句的主詞一致。

例如：

generally speaking 一般來說

given the conditions 在既定的條件下

simply put 簡單說來

to be honest (frank) with you 老實說

to tell the truth 告訴你實話

牛刀小試 ►TEST

1. The board consists of 7 members _____ by the city council.

(A) appointed   (B) appointing

(C) appoint   (D) to appoint

詳解

因為是被動的，所以由appoint的過去分詞appointed來帶出形容詞片語appointed by the council（市議會指定的）。

翻譯

董事會是由市議會指定的七個成員所組成的。

(A) 被指定的

2. _____ given birth to 4 kids, the woman still keeps in shape, looking young and fit.

(A) To have   (B) Has

(C) Had   (D) Having

詳解

因為生孩子是主動的，所以由現在分詞having given來連接兩個子句。

翻譯

　　生完四個孩子後，這個婦人仍然保持好身材，看起來年輕又健美。

　　(D) have 的現在分詞

3. The relief plans _____ by the government will come into effect on Oct. 8, 2021.

　　(A) approve　　　　(B) approved

　　(C) approves　　　 (D) approving

詳解

　　因為是被動的，所以由approve的過去分詞approved來作為形容詞。

翻譯

　　政府核准的紓困計畫會在2021年十月8日生效。

　　(B) 被核准的

4. The government rushes to contain the _____ Delta outbreak before the holidays.

　　(A) unexpecting　　(B) unexpected

　　(C) expecting　　　(D) expects

詳解

　　因為是被動的，所以由expect（期待）的過去分詞expected（期待的）作為形容詞，不被預期的，則在前面加上un，表示否定，所以要選unexpected。

翻譯

政府急忙在假期前控制住出乎意料外的Delta爆發。

(B) 出乎意料外的

5. The water _____ from washing dishes can be used to water plants.

(A) saving

(B) saves

(C) is saved

(D) saved

詳解

因為是被動的，所以由save的過去分詞saved來作為形容詞。

翻譯

洗碗省下的水可以用來澆花。

(D) 被省下的

6. We have a job vacancy _____ a person who can translate from Chinese into English and English into Chinese.

(A) requires

(B) requiring

(C) require

(D) required

詳解

　　因為是主動的，所以由require的現在分詞requiring來作為形容詞。

翻譯

　　我們有個職缺需要能英翻中、中翻英。

　　(B) 需要的現在分詞

7. **The joint project _____ by two group of experts from two prominent research institutes has brought the best result in the medical history.**

　　(A) leading 　　　　　(B) led

　　(C) lead 　　　　　　(D) leads

詳解

　　因為是被動的，所以由lead的過去分詞led來作為形容詞。

翻譯

　　由兩個傑出研究機構的專家領導的共同計劃，帶來了醫學史上的最佳結果。

　　(B) 被領導的

8. _____ under very high pressure, the staff members of the office still maintain a good sense of humor.

(A) work

(B) works

(C) worked

(D) working

詳解

因為是主動的，所以由work的現在分詞working來作為形容詞。

翻譯

在極高壓力下，辦公室的員工們仍然保持良好的幽默感。

(D) work的現在分詞

9. Tired and _____ out, the plumber tried all means to find out what might go wrong with the water pipes around the house.

(A) worked

(B) working

(C) works

(D) is working

詳解

因為是被動的，所以由work的過去分詞worked來作為形容詞，意思是被操勞的。

翻譯

　　水電工疲憊且操勞，盡最大努力來找出房子外的水管出了什麼問題。

　　(A) work 的過去分詞

10. **The most _____ but not much mentioned news is that even after taking 2 vaccines, one can still contract COVID-19.**

　　(A) shocked　　　　(B) shocking

　　(C) shocks　　　　(D) shock

詳解

　　因為是主動的，所以由 shock 的現在分詞 shocking 來作為形容詞。

翻譯

　　最驚人但卻不常為人提及的新聞是，即使打了兩劑疫苗後仍然可能染疫。

　　(B) shock 的現在分詞

●Part6 段落填空

重點提示：

Part 6 可以視為 Part 5 的進階版，基本上是一篇短文，共有 4 題，其中 3 題是單句填空，類似 Part 5，選擇最適合的單字，還有 1 題是選擇最適合插入的句子。

重點一

基本上除了 Part 5 的注意重點外，Part 6 還要特別注意一些標示出文意轉變的詞彙：

◎ 表示「轉折」

nevertheless 儘管如此

however 然而

but 但是

although 雖然

◎ 表示「而且、此外」

moreover 而且

in addition 還有

besides 此外

furthermore 再者

◎ 表示「因果」

because 因為

hence 因此

due to 由於

therefore 所以

◎ 表示「對比」

unlike 與……相反

while 儘管

nevertheless 儘管如此

重點二

插入句子

選擇最適合插入句子的難度通常頗高，因為必須要對於全文脈絡有一定程度的理解，因此經常可能需要較多的時間來作答，如果第一眼看來不是很有把握哪一句是答案，建議可以先做其它題，等全篇題目皆答完再來選擇最適合插入句子。

範例二則：

範例一：

電子郵件 E-Mail：客戶抱怨信

To: Lily Fried Chicken

From: Jennifer Jones

Date: September 21, 2022

Subject: Complaint letter

Dear Owner of Lily Fried Chicken,

Yesterday I bought a piece of breast chicken at your takeaway and was totally _____1_____ at the product. _____2_____ The breast chicken is not fresh and way too greasy. It seems that all the condiments _____3_____ cannot cover up the bad chicken flavor. In _____4_____ , its portion looks like about two third of what is usually sold at other stores. Please do improve the quality and quantity of your chicken products.

Thank you.

Your customer,

Jennifer Jones

1. (A) disappointed

   (B) disagreed

   (C) discovered

   (D) discharged

2. (A) The product is really amazing.

   (B) The chicken is worth the waiting.

   (C) The chicken does not live up to the standard of
       your brand name.

   (D) The product is much cheaper than I expected.

3. (A) using

   (B) used

   (C) can use

   (D) use

4. (A) adding

   (B) to add

   (C) addition

   (D) added

正確答案：1. A　2. C　3. B　4. C

範例二：

告示 Notice：商標侵權

Sep. 21, 2022

CUSTOMER NOTICE

Dear Customers,

As you might have _____1_____ , there is a new restaurant operating under the name of Lily fried chicken restaurant, which is too similar to our well-known brand name Lily Taiwanese restaurant. _____2_____ , the logo and packaging seem to copy our styles. We would like to remind customers that our 21-year-old restaurant do not have any related companies or chain eateries, not to _____3_____ fried chicken takeaways. Please do not confuse our restaurant with others. In the meantime, we are in the process of taking legal action against Lily fried chicken restaurant. This trademark issue is to be solved as soon as possible. _____4_____ . Thank you very much.

General Manager
Deming Chen
Lily Taiwanese Restaurant

1. (A) notice

   (B) noticed

   (C) to notice

   (D) noticing

2. (A) Besides

   (B) Beside

   (C) Aside

   (D) Apart

3. (A) talk

   (B) discuss

   (C) say

   (D) mention

4. (A) We are grateful to have you as customers.

   (B) We are sorry for any inconvenience caused by this.

   (C) We are open for suggestions of new dishes.

   (D) We are glad if you give us feedback.

正確答案：1. B　2. A　3. D　4. B

　　文法整理內容部分摘錄自拙作《秒懂！關鍵英文文法輕鬆學》，其中有針對多益文法以及Part 5 & Part 6的詳盡解說。

NEW TOEIC

Chapter **5**

破解閱讀 Part 7
各文章型式

閱讀Part7 由單篇或多篇文章組成，型式大致如下：

● Part7 文章主要分為以下幾種型式：

一、電子郵件

二、商業信件

三、新聞報導

四、廣告

五、公告／通知

六、表格

七、線上對話紀錄

● 一、電子郵件

電子郵件是商業界經常使用的溝通方式，因此於多益閱讀測驗可說是必定會出現的題型。請注意以下幾點：

1. 確認寄件者（From:）＆收件者（To:）

寄件者與收件者的電子郵件地址如果有明列，可以略知所屬的公司與國家；收件者的職稱與寄件者的簽名檔（職稱、公司名稱、地址）都是很好的線索，可以推論得知彼此的關係。

2. 確認主題（Subject: 或 Re:）

Subject 是主題，Re則是Regarding（關於）的縮寫，好的主題可以讓人對於內容一目了然，節省不少閱讀時間。

附帶一提，如果Subject: 或Re: 的欄內如果出現Re：則表示Reply，表示「回覆」，不要與Regarding（關於）弄混了。

3. 確認日期（Date:）

日期經常會是測驗的重點，特別是在多篇閱讀時，可能需要參考日期才能找到關於時間的正確答案。

4. 確認第一段與最後一段大意

通常電子郵件的第一段會概述全文內容大意，而其中第一段的第一二句就會點明主題；最後一段則經常會提到後續如何處理，所以也是考試重點。

範例

Questions XXX—XXX refer to the following e-mail.

To: Mr. James Chen

From: Kevin Wang

Date: Oct. 29, 2022

Subject: Application: Interior Designer

Dear Mr. Chen,

In the online Design Newsletter, it is stated you are looking for a new interior designer for your design studio. I have been in the field of private housing and garden designing for the past four years as a freelance designer. My works have won several awards, which is uncommon for a young designer. I find my style of simplicity fits in very well with the works of your studio, and that's why I think I am a suitable candidate for this position. If you have time to give me an interview, I'd be glad to present you the work portfolio. In the attachments you can find the references of my previous employers. Thank you and I look forward to having the opportunity to work with you.

Best regards,

Kevin Wang

1. What's the purpose of this e-mail?

(A) To apply for scholarship.

(B) To apply for a work visa.

(C) To apply for a research project.

(D) To apply for a position.

2. What type of company is Mr. Chen probably in charge of?

(A) A construction company.

(B) An interior design studio.

(C) An English school.

(D) A real estate company.

3. What makes Kevin Wang think he fits in with Mr. Chen's studio?

(A) His design wins Mr. Chen's approval.

(B) His construction models receive international awards.

(C) His made a great impression on Mr. Chen

(D) His previous works suit Mr. Chen's style.

4. Why does Kevin Wang want to meet up with Mr. Chen?

(A) To present his portfolio.

(B) To take him to a construction site.

(C) To ask him to write a reference for him.

(D) To talk with him about some new ideas.

5. What might be the attachments?

(A) Sketches of design.

(B) Blueprint of a building.

(C) Reference letters.

(D) Resumes.

To: 陳建銘先生
From: 王愷文
Date: 2022 年 10 月 29 日
Subject: 求職：室內設計師

陳先生　您好：

　　您在線上設計電子報刊載說貴室內設計公司在徵求一位新室內設計師，我過去四年一直從事私人住宅與庭院作品設計的自由接案工作。我得到多項獎項，這一點對一個年輕設計師來說很難得。我認為我的極簡風格與貴設計公司的作品非常吻合，所以我認為自己是這個職缺的合適人選。如果您能撥空給我一個面試機會，我會很樂意帶我的作品集給您參考，在此電子郵件的附件內，您可以看見我之前雇主的推薦信。非常感謝您，期待有榮幸為您服務。

王愷文　敬上

---

1. 這封電子郵件的目的為何？

(A) 申請獎學金。

(B) 申請工作簽證。

(C) 申請研究專案。

(D) 求職。

2. 陳先生可能是什麼樣的公司的負責人？

(A) 建設公司。

(B) 室內設計公司。

(C) 英語學校。

(D) 房地產公司。

3. 為什麼王愷文認為他適合陳先生的設計公司？

(A) 他的作品贏得陳先生的肯定。

(B) 他的建築模型獲得國際獎項。

(C) 他留給陳先生良好的印象。

(D) 他之前的作品符合陳先生的風格。

4. 為什麼王愷文想要與陳先生會面？

(A) 為了提供作品集。

(B) 帶他去工地。

(C) 請他為自己寫推薦信。

(D) 與他討論一些新點子。

5. 附件可能是什麼？

(A) 設計草圖。

(B) 建築藍圖。

(C) 推薦信。

(D) 履歷表。

正確答案：

　　1. D　2. B　3. D　4. A　5. C

●二、商業信件

通常商業

　　商業信件通常較電子郵件內容較長且較為正式，要注意的重點如下：

1. 確認信件的寄件人與收件人

　　信件的寄件人名＆地址寫於信件的左上方，空一格，寫日期，再空一格，寫收件人稱謂＆姓名與地址，(請見範例)，再空一格，開始寫信件內容。

2. 常問此封商業信件的目的為何？因為商業信件較長，可能開始一二句會是寒暄等開場白，所以相較於電子郵件可能要多讀一點才能得知全信目的。

順便一提常用的正式英文書信結尾：

Best regards

Regards

Respectfully

Respectfully yours

Yours respectfully

Sincerely

Sincerely yours

Yours sincerely

Yours truly

Truly yours

範例

Jerry Smith

Kent College

27 Kent St.

Bankstown 2991

Australia

Oct. 30, 2022

Leopard Headhunter

No. 201

Zhongxiao East Rd. Sec 4

Taipei, Taiwan

To Whom it May Concern,

In light of the new trend of Chinese learning in Australia, our college has decided to offer Chinese to students who select the language to learn. We are currently looking for two Chinese teachers for remote learning modes. Interested candidates should have previous teaching experiences related to language teaching. Initially, all candidates have to pass an interview online to see if their personalities suit the position. Afterwards, a 45-minute class demonstration will be required of each candidate and will be conducted in teleconferencing mode with our teaching team members. We trust you can help us find the right teachers efficiently. Thank you for your assistance in advance.

Yours sincerely,
Jerry Smith

1. **What is the main purpose of this business letter?**

   (A) To inquire about the Chinese courses.

   (B) To ask for Chinese translators.

   (C) To set up an online language school.

   (D) To look for Chinese teachers abroad.

2. **What is the closest meaning of the phrase "in light of" in the first line?**

   (A) In consideration of.

   (B) In addition to.

   (C) In contrast of.

   (D) In condition of.

3. **How will the classes be conducted?**

   (A) Students learn in a classroom.

   (B) Students learn from remote teaching.

   (C) Students learn with ESL books with CDs.

   (D) Students learn with audial visual aids.

4. **What does the writer specifically require of the candidates from the headhunter?**

(A) The candidates should have a B.A. in education.

(B) The candidates should major in Chinese.

(C) The candidates should have a B.A. in language teaching.

(D) The candidates should have previous teaching experiences.

5. **Besides an interview, what do the candidates have to do in order to get the job?**

(A) Doing a class demonstration.

(B) Submitting teaching materials.

(C) Providing Police Criminal Record Certificate.

(D) Providing a teaching certificate.

肯特學院
肯特街27號
班克斯鎮2991
澳洲

2022年10月30日

花豹獵頭公司
台灣台北市忠孝東路四段201號

敬啟者：

　　考量到澳洲學中文的新潮流，我們學院決定提供中文給選修這個語言來學習的學生，我們目前在徵求兩位遠距教學的中文老師，有興趣的應徵者之前必須要有語言教學的經驗，首先所有的應徵者必須通過線上面試來判斷他們的個性是否符合這個職位，然後每位應徵者都要做45分鐘的示範教學，而且必須要以視訊模式與我們教學團隊成員來進行，我相信您一定能有效率地幫我們找到適合的老師，預先感謝您的協助。

傑瑞史密斯

敬上

1. 這封商業信件的主要目的是什麼？

(A) 詢問中文課程。

(B) 尋找中文翻譯員。

(C) 成立一間線上語言學校。

(D) 徵求海外中文教師。

2. 第一行"**in light of**"這個片語最接近什麼意思？

(A) 考量……。

(B) 除了……之外。

(C) 對比……。

(D) ……條件下。

3. 課程會以什麼方式進行？

(A) 學生在教室學習。

(B) 學生以遠距教學方式學習。

(C) 學生以英語教學書籍和CD學習。

(D) 學生以視聽輔助教材學習。

4. 寫信者特別要求獵頭公司什麼樣的人選？

(A) 求職者必須有教育學士學位。

(B) 求職者必須要主修中文。

(C) 求職者必須要有語言教學學士。

(D) 求職者必須要有先前教學經驗。

5. 除了面試，求職者必須要做什麼才能得到這份工作？

(A) 做示範教學。

(B) 提供教材。

(C) 提供良民證。

(D) 提供教師證。

正確答案：

1. D　2. A　3. B　4. D　5. A

●三、新聞報導

　　新聞報導可以算是閱讀文體當中比較難的一種，不像電子郵件和商業信件有那麼固定的形式，也考驗考生的閱讀實力，第一段的第一二句經常是主旨所在，如果有分段的話，先略讀每段的第一二句可以有助於快速了解每段大意，但是如果並沒有分段，就要靠一些閱讀技巧，來判別文章語氣的轉變，才能高效率理解報導文意的起承轉合。

範例

Taiwan to partially ease outdoor mask mandate from Oct. 5

TAIPEI (Taiwan News) — Central Epidemic Command Center (CECC) head Chen Shih-chung announced on Sunday (Oct. 3) that starting from Tuesday, people in Taiwan will no longer be required to wear masks in wide-open spaces in outdoor environments.

Chen cited farm fields, fishponds, beaches, and forests and mountains, including forest recreation areas as examples of such environments. Riversides and outdoor hot springs are not included in this round of restriction easing though. It remains unclear as to what belongs to the category of the wide-open spaces. The reason for this easing of mask requirement outdoors is probably that the numbers of the confirmed local COVID-19 cases have remained near zero since the Mid-Autumn Festival holiday (Sept. 21) .

1. What is the general topic of the news in Taiwan?

(A) Mask requirement outdoors will be lifted.

(B) Vaccination is mandatory.

(C) The COVID-19 pass is coming.

(D) Mask wearing is outdated.

2. In which of the following place does one have to wear a mask?

(A) Fishponds.

(B) Mountains.

(C) Forests.

(D) Hot spring.

3. What is the definition of the wide-open spaces category?

(A) National parks.

(B) Forest parks.

(C) No clear definition.

(D) All parks.

4. According to this passage, what probably brings about this partial outdoor mask easing?

(A) The vaccination has worked among adults.

(B) The cure of COVID-19 has been found in the lab.

(C) Masks do not have the protection against COVID-19.

(D) The numbers of confirmed COVID-19 cases have stayed almost zero.

台灣將從10月5日起有條件放寬戶外戴口罩規定

　　台北（台灣英文新聞）— 中央疫情指揮中心指揮官陳時中於10月3日星期日宣布，在台灣戶外空曠地方將不需要戴口罩。

　　陳舉例像是農圃、魚池、海灘、森林、山上，包含森林遊樂園區，皆是屬於這類地區，河邊和戶外溫泉不包含在這一輪解禁範圍內，至於什麼是戶外空曠地方的定義不甚清楚，解除戴口罩禁令的原因可能是從中秋節（9月21日）以來，新冠肺炎的確診人數保持接近零。

1. 這則關於台灣的新聞大意是什麼？

   (A) 戶外將不必戴口罩。

   (B) 接種疫苗是強制性的。

   (C) 新冠疫苗護照來臨了。

   (D) 戴口罩是過時的。

2. 在下列哪個地方必須要戴口罩？

   (A) 魚池。

   (B) 山上。

   (C) 森林。

   (D) 溫泉。

3. 什麼是戶外空曠地方的定義？

   (A) 國家公園。

   (B) 森林公園。

   (C) 定義不明。

   (D) 所有公園。

4. 根據這篇文章，什麼可能是戴口罩禁令部分解除的原因？

   (A) 疫苗於成人已經見效。

   (B) 新冠肺炎的解藥已經於實驗室研發出來。

(C) 口罩對於對抗新冠肺炎無效。

(D) 新冠肺炎的確診人數保持接近零。

正確答案：

1. A　2. D　3. C　4. D

四、廣告

1. 標題

　　廣告的標題通常都會很明確告知是旅館或百貨週年慶活動，或是宣傳商品或服務等等。

2. 大意在標題和開頭數行

　　開頭通常就是大意所在，廣告為了吸引顧客注意力，通常會寫得非常明確。

3. 先略讀題目做好準備再來搜尋所需的訊息，會比較快找到答案。

4. 注意數字

　　例如：日期、星期、其它數字，以及地點，例如早鳥價等的特價活動，何時開始何時結束、折扣優惠、退換貨日期等等。

5. 注意小文字

　　如同合約，廣告的小文字就像但書，例如化妝品買一送一，其實可能是買一大瓶的某產品，附送另外產品一小瓶，不可不留意。

範例

　　With modern and warm examination environment and professional team, the Ming De Hospital provides health checkups with detailed examination, accurate reports and follow-up consultation to monitor patients' health conditions.

　　Ming De hospital is among the few medical institutions that can help apply for visas for people from Mainland China to receive a physical examination or cosmetic medical procedures. Recently, the plastic surgeries the hospital offers are particularly popular among both locals and medical tourists.

　　Aside from the cosmetic medical treatment, altogether 10 packages of health checkups are offered to people with their special requests of physical conditions. Please make a phone call and the specialists can explain to you as to which package suits you best or answer any questions you might have. Alternatively, you can consult the service clerk at the service counter at the following address.

Mon. to Fri.   9:00 am 17:00 pm

Tel: 886-2-2323 4545

E-mail: check@health.com.tw

Address: No. 252, Dunghua North Rd. Taipei

1. What is the advertisement mainly for?

(A) Health seminars.

(B) Health checkups.

(C) Chinese physicians.

(D) Senior citizens' health.

2. What group of people is especially mentioned here as the interested group of health checkups and cosmetic medical services of the hospital?

(A) Cosmetic surgeons from Korea.

(B) International exchange researchers.

(C) Chinese medical tourist groups.

(D) Special medical experts from China.

3. **Which of the following is mentioned here especially as the recent popular medical service?**

   (A) Herbal medicine and acupuncture.

   (B) Orthopedic surgeries.

   (C) Diabetes and nutrition.

   (D) Cosmetic surgeries.

4. **What are the possible items included in the packages?**

   (A) Specific items of health examinations.

   (B) Special payments.

   (C) Nutrition advice.

   (D) Extra health supplements.

5. **According to this article, which of the following is NOT one of the ways to make an appointment?**

   (A) Phone call.

   (B) Fax.

   (C) Dropping by.

   (D) E-mail.

明德醫院的檢驗環境現代且讓人舒適，團隊專業，所提供的健康檢查不但詳細而且報告準確，還有之後的諮詢，以追蹤病患的健康狀況。

　　明德醫院是能為中國大陸人民申請健康檢查或醫美簽證的少數醫療機構，最近醫院所提供的整型手術特別受到當地人與醫療觀光團的喜愛。

　　除了醫美服務，總共有10個健康檢查的套裝健檢服務，讓有不同健康狀況特殊需求的人來選擇。請撥個電話，讓專員來為您解釋哪一種套裝健檢服務最適合您，或是解答任何您可能有的問題。不然的話，您也可以到以下地址的服務台詢問服務員。

星期一至星期五　早上 9 點至下午 5 點

電話：886-2-2323 4545

電子郵件地址：check@health.com.tw

地址：台北市敦化北路252號

1. 這個廣告主要目的為何？

   (A) 健康講座。

   (B) 健檢服務。

   (C) 中國醫師。

   (D) 銀髮族健康。

2. 哪一類人是這裡所特別提到，對於醫院的健檢與醫美
   服務感到有興趣的人？

   (A) 韓國來的整型醫師。

   (B) 國際交換研究員。

   (C) 中國醫療觀光團。

   (D) 中國來的特別醫療專家。

3. 下列何者是最近流行的醫療服務項目？

   (A) 中藥和針灸。

   (B) 骨科手術。

   (C) 糖尿病和營養。

   (D) 整型手術。

4. 在套裝健檢服務內可能是什麼項目？

   (A) 特別的健康檢查項目。

   (B) 特別費用。

   (C) 營養建議。

   (D) 額外的健康補品。

5. 根據這篇文章，下列何者不是預約的方式之一？

(A) 電話。

(B) 傳真。

(C) 路過詢問。

(D) 電子郵件。

正確答案：

1. B　2. C　3. D　4. A　5. B

●五、公告／通知

　　不同於廣告是以商業利益為目的，公告或通知是以某特定族群為對象，發布某訊息，例如公司對員工、公司對客戶、管委會對住戶進行公共事項（停電或施工等等）的佈達。

　　(1) 注意標題和副標題等醒目字體。

　　(2) 先略讀題目做好準備再來搜尋所需的訊息，會比較快找到答案。

　　(3) 要多留意公告或通知類文章內所出現的數字、日期、時間。

Questions XXX—XXX refer to the following notice.

Here's what to know about the Quintuple Stimulus Vouchers

Premier Su Tseng-chang announced on Thursday that the Quintuple Stimulus Vouchers are scheduled to be launched during the National Day long weekend starting on Oct. 8.

Who can get them?

Any Taiwanese citizen can obtain the vouchers and use them from Oct. 8 to until April 30, 2022. Foreign spouses with permanent residency in Taiwan (ARC) , and foreigners with Alien Permanent Resident Certificate are eligible too.

How to get them?

If you are planning to acquire vouchers through convenience stores, you can register on Sept. 25 and acquire them on Oct. 8 as well. You can register for the digital stimulus vouchers via credit cards, e-tickets, and mobile payment apps, starting on Sept. 22. If you prefer the postal service, you need to register on Oct. 4. You will obtain the vouchers a bit later — on Oct. 12. The timing of receiving the vouchers is well planned to avoid disorder. Under no circumstances should the stimulus vouchers be used in exchange for cash. Unlike previous year, no need to pay NT$1,000 first to obtain the vouchers. All you need to do is to apply for them online here: http://5000.gov.tw/

What will the vouchers look like?

This year's quintuple vouchers package will include three vouchers at NT$1,000, two at NT$500, and five at NT$200.

Where can I use it?

Almost all stores will accept stimulus vouchers, including quite a few selected e-commerce platforms. Stimulus vouchers will not be applicable for water fees, electricity fees, fines, labor insurance payments, health insurance payments, and national pension insurance payments.

1. **How can the eligible people get the stimulus vouchers?**

   (A) Through lottery draws.

   (B) In convenience stores and post offices.

   (C) By downloading apps from the official website.

   (D) By applying to the Ministry of Economics.

2. **Why is the timing for people receiving stimulus vouchers so scheduled?**

   (A) So that there will not be crowds in getting vouchers.

   (B) So that people can use stimulus vouchers for various purposes.

   (C) So that it will benefit as many industries as possible.

   (D) So that nobody can take advantage of others.

3. **What should the stimulus vouchers never be used to do?**

   (A) To obtain real money.

   (B) To pay for concert tickets.

   (C) To buy items in a supermarket.

   (D) To pay for postage.

4. **Compared to last year, what is the biggest difference in obtaining the stimulus vouchers this year?**

   (A) One can exchange the stimulus vouchers for money this year.

   (B) One does not have to pay NT$1000 in advance this year.

   (C) One has 2 years to use the stimulus vouchers this year.

   (D) One can pay for national health insurance with the stimulus vouchers this year.

5. **Which one in the following is NOT applicable for the use of the Quintuple Stimulus Vouchers?**

   (A) Stands at night markets.

   (B) Traffic fines.

   (C) Selected e-commerce stores.

   (D) Supermarkets.

五倍券須知

台北《英文中國郵報》— 行政院長蘇貞昌星期四公布預計於 10 月 8 日國慶日連假開始發放五倍券。

誰能得到五倍券？

所有的台灣公民都可以得到五倍券，使用日期為 10 月 8 日至 2022 年 4 月 30 日，擁有永久居住權的外籍配偶以及持有台灣永久居留證的外國人都符合資格可以得到五倍券。

如何得到五倍券？

如果您計畫於超商取得五倍券，您也可以在 9 月 25 日登記，在 10 月 8 日領取；9 月 22 日起您可以用信用卡、電子票證、電子支付來登記五倍券；如果您比較喜歡用郵政服務，您就必須在 10 月 4 日登記，領取五倍券時間則稍晚 10 月 12 日。領取五倍券的時間是有計畫安排的，以避免混亂。五倍券絕對不可以用來換現金。不同於去年，領取五倍券前不需先預付 1000 元，只需上官網申請：http://5000.gov.tw/。

五倍券看起來什麼樣子？

今年的五倍券會有 3 張 1000 元、2 張 500 元、5 張 200 元。

我可以在哪裡使用五倍券？

幾乎所有的商店都會使用五倍券，包含不少家特定的電子商業平台。五倍券不可用來付水電費、罰款、勞保健保費、國民年金費。

1. 符合資格的人要如何得到五倍券？

(A) 經由抽獎。

(B) 於超商和郵局。

(C) 由官網下載App。

(D) 向經濟部申請。

2. 為什麼得到五倍券的時間如此安排？

(A) 避免人們為了得到五倍券而擁擠。

(B) 好方便人們將五倍券用於不同的目的。

(C) 好讓更多產業獲利。

(D) 才不會有人圖利於他人。

3. 五倍券絕對不可以用來做什麼？

(A) 換取現金。

(B) 買音樂會的票。

(C) 在超市買東西。

(D) 付郵資。

4. 相較於去年，今年領取五倍券最大的不同處何在？

(A) 今年可以用五倍券來換現金。

(B) 今年不用預付1000元。

(C) 今年五倍券有兩年的使用期限。

(D) 今年可以使用五倍券來付國民健保。

5. 下列哪一項不得使用五倍券？

(A) 夜市的攤販。

(B) 交通罰款。

(C) 特定的電子商店。

(D) 超市。

正確答案：

　　1. B　2. A　3. D　4. B　5. B

意見調查表

　　意見調查表算是簡易表格的一種，目的是為了要蒐集大量的回饋意見，來統整某些特定的訊息，現在的醫院、餐廳、銀行都會有這類意見調查表，只要日常生活中多留意這些表格的英文版，就可以增加熟悉度。

　　注意標題和副標題等醒目字體。

　　先略讀題目做好準備再來搜尋所需的訊息，會比較快找到答案。

　　意見調查表就如同很多表格一樣，不需要細讀，重點在於迅速掌握表格的功能，理解數字和圖示背後的意義。

範例

Customer Satisfaction Survey with Online Banking

1. Gender

● Female

○ Male

○ Other

2. Your age range

○ 18—30 years old

○ 30—40 years old

● 40—50 years old

○ 50—60 years old

○ 60—70 years old

○ above 70 years old

3. How long have you been using our digital banking?

○ under 6 months

○ 6 months—1 year

● 1—3 years

○ 3—5 years

○ more than 5 years

4. Please rate your level of agreement with the following statements about our website and using your account online.

	Strongly Disagree	Disagree	Neutral	Agree	Strongly Agree
The website works well technically				√	
Information is clear and complete				√	
It is easy to navigate and manage					√
My online account works well				√	
My online account meets my needs			√		

5. Please rate your satisfaction level with your recent experience of online banking with our company.

○ Very Dissatisfied

○ Dissatisfied

○ Neutral

● Satisfied

○ Very Satisfied

6. What are your main reasons for using our online banking?

efficiency in time and efforts, latest update of banking products

7. Would you recommend a friend or colleague to use our mobile baking?

Yes, because it is quite reliable.

8. Please provide any feedback you would like us to know.

Please send me an e-mail after each transaction.

1. **What is the general purpose of this questionnaire?**

   (A) To collect the information of products.

   (B) To collect the feedback of online banking.

   (C) To collect the problems of website of the bank.

   (D) To collect the input of the bank representatives.

2. **In which aspect related to banking does the questionnaire want to find out most?**

   (A) Gender of the customers.

   (B) Age range of the customers.

   (C) Customers' experiences of online banking.

   (D) Special needs of the female customers.

3. **In using her account online, what does the customer find especially good about the online banking?**

   (A) The information is not updated.

   (B) It is hard to keep informed of the products.

   (C) The online accounts are hard to read.

   (D) The online banking system is easy to use.

4. Which is the following is NOT one of the main reasons for the customer to use digital banking?

(A) It saves time.

(B) It saves trouble.

(C) The information of products.

(D) The bank tellers are helpful.

5. What suggestions does the customer provide?

(A) Please send her an e-mail of details after each transaction.

(B) Please inform her of the latest exchange rate.

(C) Please do not send her letter of statements.

(D) Please send her a summary in the end of year.

網路銀行客戶滿意意見調查表

1. 性別

● 女

○ 男

○ 其他

2. 您的年級範圍

○ 18—30 歲

○ 30—40 歲

● 40—50 歲

○ 50—60 歲

○ 60—70 歲

○ 70 歲以上

3. 您使用我們的網路銀行有多久了？

○ 6 個月以下

○ 6 個月—1 年

● 1—3 年

○ 3—5 年

○ 5 年以上

4. 請對以下關於我們網路和您使用網路帳戶的描述評分。

	Strongly Disagree	Disagree	Neutral	Agree	Strongly Agree
網站運作非常良好				√	
資訊清楚且完整				√	
很容易瀏覽、管理					√
我的網路帳戶運作良好				√	
我的網路帳戶符合我的需求				√	

5. 請對關於您在我們公司網路銀行的最近經驗滿意程度評分。

○ 非常不滿意

○ 不滿意

○ 中性

● 滿意

○ 非常滿意

6. 您使用我們網路銀行的主要原因為何？

省時省事、銀行產品的最新資訊。

7. 您會推薦朋友或同事使用我們的網路銀行嗎？

會，因為很可靠。

8. 請提供您想讓我們知道的回饋意見。

請於每筆交易後寄給我一封電子信件。

1. 這個意見調查表的主要目的為何？

(A) 收集產品的資訊。

(B) 收集網路銀行的回饋意見。

(C) 收集銀行網頁的問題。

(D) 收集銀行業務代表的輸入資料。

2. 這個意見調查表最想要得到關於銀行的哪方面資訊？

(A) 客戶的性別。

(B) 客戶的年紀範圍。

(C) 客戶使用網路銀行的經驗。

(D) 女性客戶的特別需求。

3. 這位客戶在使用網路帳戶時，有什麼覺得有什麼特別好的地方？

(A) 資訊沒有更新。

(B) 無法跟上產品資訊的更新。

(C) 網路帳戶很難讀懂。

(D) 網路銀行系統很容易使用。

4. 下列的哪一個原因不是客戶使用網路銀行的主要原因？

(A) 節省時間。

(B) 省事。

(C) 產品資訊。

(D) 銀行櫃員很熱心。

5. 這位客戶提出了什麼建議？

(A) 請於每次交易後寄給她明細的電子郵件。

(B) 請告知她最新的匯率。

(C) 請不要寄聲明書給她。

(D) 請每年年底寄給她。

正確答案：

1. B　2. C　3. D　4. D　5. A

● 七、線上對話紀錄

　　線上聊天的題型在兩人交談時，通常都很容易，如果有三人或以上的話，則要多注意是誰說了什麼話，尤其是誰姓什麼與名字叫什麼，要能對得起來，有時可能考題出現的是某先生，但是在線上對話紀錄上顯現的是他的名字。除此之外，還要注意：

　　每句對話通常都不長，對話常常是跳躍式的，人數一多更可能無法很快理解內容，因此不容易迅速找到答案，請不要小看這類題型。

　　因為是對話所以使用英語口語用法機會增多，經常會測驗某人在某時間說了什麼，他想要問的是什麼。

範例

Amy

Do you guys know KTV reopened yesterday?

John

Let's go together after work!

Vicky

But I heard masks must be worn at all times, including singing with a microphone.

Amy

And no eating or drinking, except water.

John

It doesn't matter. I haven't been singing at a KTV for a long time.

Amy

It should be quite safe. For contact tracing, all customers have to scan QR codes twice.

Vicky

Once before entering the main entrance, and the second time upon going into the rooms.

Amy

The police are doing random checks to make sure the rules are followed.

John

What are you waiting for? I'll pick you two up at 6 o'clock sharp.

1. What is the main topic of the conversation?

(A) Going to a concert.

(B) Practicing in a chorus.

(C) Going to a KTV.

(D) Food good for singing.

2. What is the biggest concern of their discussion?

(A) Police random checks.

(B) The costs of entrance fees.

(C) The food and drinks.

(D) Safety of singing there.

3. What is the purpose of scanning 2 QR codes?

(A) To see if customers are vaccinated.

(B) To enforce contact tracing.

(C) To check if customers have done PCR.

(D) To make sure customers do not eat and sing.

4. What is done in order to ensure that nobody violates the KTV regulations?

(A) Police random checks.

(B) Customer advance booking.

(C) Background check.

(D) Reports of KTV staff.

5. What does John mean with "6 o'clock sharp"?

(A) The girls must be punctual.

(B) The girls must prepare masks.

(C) The girls must bring water.

(D) The girls must practice singing.

艾美

你們知道KTV昨天重新開張了嗎？

約翰

我們下班後一起去吧！

薇琪

但是我聽說必須要全程戴口罩，包含對著麥克風唱歌的時候。

艾美

而且不准吃東西或喝飲料，除了水以外。

約翰

沒關係啦，我已經很久沒有去KTV唱歌了。

艾美

應該很安全，所有的客人都必須掃描QR code兩次以配合實聯制。

薇琪

進大門的時候掃描一次，進包廂時掃描第二次。

艾美

警察會抽查以確保大家遵循這些規定。

約翰

還等什麼呢？六點整我來接妳們。

1. 這段對話的主題是什麼？

   (A) 去聽音樂會。

   (B) 合唱團練唱。

   (C) 去KTV。

   (D) 有助唱歌的食物。

2. 他們討論的最大顧慮是什麼？

   (A) 警察抽查。

   (B) 入場券費用。

   (C) 食物和飲料。

   (D) 在那裡唱歌的安全。

3. 掃描兩次 **QR code** 的目的是什麼？

   (A) 看看客人是否接種了疫苗。

   (B) 加強實聯制。

   (C) 檢查客人是否做了PCR。

   (D) 確保客人不邊吃邊唱歌。

4. 為了確保沒有人不遵守**KTV**規定，有什麼做法？

(A) 警察抽查。

(B) 客人提前預約。

(C) 背景調查。

(D) KTV人員舉報。

5. 約翰說的 "**6 o'clock sharp**" 是什麼意思？

(A) 女孩們必須要準時。

(B) 女孩們必須要準備口罩。

(C) 女孩們必須要帶水。

(D) 女孩們必須要練習唱歌。

正確答案：

1. C　2. D　3. B　4. A　5. A

兩篇／多篇為以上組合，常以下列形式出現

> Questions XX－XX refer to the following ＿＿＿
> and ＿＿＿.

廣告 advertisement

電子郵件 e-mail

信件 letter

文章 article

報導 report

文件 document

使用說明 instruction

公告／通知 notice

表格 form

清單 list

費用清單 invoice

線上對話紀錄 online exchanges

NEW TOEIC

Chapter **6**

破解閱讀 Part 7
各考題型式

●Part 7 考題主要有以下幾種型式：

一、整篇／多篇文章大意

二、關鍵字　key words (scan, skim)

三、細節　5W (who, what, where, when, how)

四、NOT

五、同義字／片語

六、插入句子

七、延伸文義

八、交叉比對　（多篇）

●解題技巧

先看題目再看文章

　　看了題目再看文章，你會更快理解文章情境。注意文章形式，是信件還是廣告？該文章又是寫給誰看？這些都是考試重點。

速讀

(略讀skimming & 掃讀scanning)

速讀需要瀏覽技巧，依照所搜尋內容不同分為略讀和掃讀：

略讀：搜尋較為籠統的大意，詢問整篇文章大意要用略讀，例如問說寫這封電子郵件的人目的是什麼。

掃讀：搜尋特定的細節資訊則要用掃讀，先看題目的關鍵字的是who, what, where, when, how，掌握好目標掃描全文來快速找的答案。常見的關鍵字有：數字、職務、場所、日期、行程、次數、費用。

同義詞和換句話說

文章內的字彙和片語在題目與選項中，不會用完全一樣的形式出現，平時就要注意不同表達方式，例如同義字和換句話說。

● 常出現的題型：

一、整篇／多篇文章大意

這一類的題目答案通常在第一段的第一二句就可以找到答案，不然的話只要略讀每段的第一二句就可以知道整片文章的大意，不需要細讀整篇文章也能輕易找到大旨。

例題

What is the article about?

What is the main purpose of the e-mail?

二、關鍵字　key words

題目詢問某特定資訊，例如：為何這個專案延宕多時？核對四個選項在文章中是否提到，快速對比一下即可得知正確答案。

例題

What is the reason that caused the one-week delay?

三、細節　5W1H: who, what, where, when, why, how (how much, how often, how big…)

此類的問題有些與以上關鍵字重疊，但是重點在測驗細項，有時候答案需要一點計算或推論才得到正確答案，例如讀到某人辦公室可能在廁所旁又靠近大門，那麼如果用平面圖來問說他的辦公房可能是哪一間，就可輕而易舉選出答案了。

例題

Where is probably his office in the map?

How much would be charged if the customer does not comply with the rules?

四、NOT

以下哪一個不符合…… 這也可算是考 " 列舉 " 的題目。多益的NOT通常都會大寫，所以應該並不會有看錯的可能性。

例題

What is NOT one of the problems the manager is facing right now?

五、同義字／片語

這種考單字或片語意義的題目，通常以下列問句出現：" What is the closest meaning of XXX?" 既然是問在這裡最接近的意思，就要找出符合上下文的用法，有時單字或片語可能有多種意義，還是需要仔細辨別出最適合的答案。

例題

What is the closest meaning of "get rid of" in the last paragraph?

(fire somebody)

六、插入句子

插入句子在考情境的上下文,這種題目難度在於,可能會有多個地方都看似可以放入所要插入的句子,但既然是要選最適合之處,空格的前後句自然都要納入考量,段落開端與結尾也非常重要,都可提供插入句子所需的線索。

例題

In which of the following positions marked [1], [2], [3] and [4] does the following sentence best belong?

Some suppliers cannot afford to provide us materials due to the rising costs of transportation, especially with ports.

七、延伸文義

通常題目型式為:" What is suggested about…?" 這類問延伸文義題目可以簡稱為推論題,也就是說,所問的題目答案通常無法於文章中找到一模一樣的答案,而是需要經過推論而得到的結論。

例題

What is suggested about the new project?

What can be inferred from this analysis of the costs?

八、交叉比對（多篇）

　　多篇閱讀測驗，特別是在兩篇或三篇，甚至多了圖表的四篇，所要找的答案常常需要於兩處或多處對比而得，掌握關鍵字當然非常重要，因為事先知道要掃讀的目標，才能針對目的來快速找尋所要的解答。

NEW TOEIC

Chapter **7**

閱讀 Part 7
模擬試題

單篇

Questions XXX—XXX refer to the following advertisement.

廣告：線上英語課程

Questions 1～5 refer to the following advertisement.

(1)

Are you a professional working in a multinational company, looking for ways to be able to read and understand English better? If you would like to improve English for your career, then this Business English Course is the best choice for you! It will help you communicate better in professional situations.

This intermediate-level English course contains 30 lessons focusing on essential vocabulary and practical phrases for the workplace. There are also plenty of exercises to help you practice your Business English!

The course is divided into four sections:

Business English Basics

◆ Vocabulary for daily uses

◆ English for interviews

◆ Talking with colleagues

◆ Phone calls

◆ Giving presentations

Business English Topics

◆ English for meetings and negotiations

◆ Business Letters & e-mails

◆ English for management & customer service

◆ Customized corporate training

Business English Specializations

◆ English for computers

◆ Legal issues

◆ Non-profit organizations

◆ Entrepreneurship

Please download our app to read further information of our company. For early bird discounts before December 1, 2021, please call 0800-030-556. If you have any inquiries, please feel free to send us an e-mail. We are more than happy to assist you in any way we can.

1. **What group of people is this advertisement most likely targeted at?**

   (A) People who just start to learn English as a beginner.

   (B) People who has never been to an English-speaking country.

   (C) People who want to communicate better in English for their jobs.

   (D) People who are bored at workplace and want to find something to do.

2. **What level of English does the business course require of students?**

   (A) intermediate.

   (B) near native level.

   (C) native.

   (D) no requirement.

3. **What does "customized corporate training" mean here?**

   (A) tailor-made business English course.

   (B) Exam preparatory course.

   (C) Everyday conversation course.

   (D) Leadership training course.

4. **What is NOT one of the business areas the English course can specialize in?**

(A) NGO.

(B) IT management.

(C) Start-up business.

(D) privatization.

5. **What should people who want early bird discounts do?**

(A) Write an e-mail.

(B) Call before a certain date.

(C) Download an app.

(D) Stop by the company.

您是在跨國公司服務的專業人士，想要增進閱讀和英文理解能力嗎？如果您想要改善您的職場英文，那麼這個商業英文課程是您的最佳選擇！課程可以幫您在專業情形溝通更良好。

　　這套共有 30 課，中等程度的英文課程著重於職場最重要字彙和實用片語，同時有很多練習來幫助您練習商業英文！

　　這個課程分為四個部分：

基本商業英文

◆ 日常字彙

◆ 英文面試

◆ 與同事聊天

◆ 電話

◆ 做簡報

商業英文主題

◆ 會議和協商英文

◆ 商業信函與電子郵件

◆ 管理與客戶服務英文

◆ 客製化企業訓練

特別商業英文

◆ 電腦英文

◆ 法律事項

◆ 非營利組織

◆ 創業家

請下載我們的App來閱讀公司的進一步資訊，想要獲得 12 月 1 日前的早鳥價，請打 0800-030-556，如有任何問題可以隨時寫電子郵件給我們，我們會非常樂意協助您。

1. 這則廣告最可能是以什麼族群為目標？

   (A) 剛開始學英文的人。

   (B) 從來沒有去過英語系國家的人。

   (C) 想要在職場上能用英文溝通更良好的人。

   (D) 在工作時感到無聊想找件事做的人。

2. 這課程對學生的英文要求為何？

   (A) 中等。

   (B) 接近母語等級。

   (C) 母語者。

   (D) 沒有要求。

3.「客製化企業訓練」在這裡是什麼意思？

   (A) 客製商業英文課程。

   (B) 準備考試課程。

   (C) 日常對話課程。

   (D) 領導人訓練課程。

4. 以下哪個商業領域不是這套英文課程特別著重的？

(A) 非營利組織。

(B) 資訊科技管理。

(C) 新創事業。

(D) 私人化。

5. 想要早鳥價的人要怎麼做？

(A) 寫一封電子郵件。

(B) 在某個日期前打電話。

(C) 下載一個App。

(D) 到公司一趟。

Questions 6～10 refer to the following notice.

(2)

Fake News about COVID-19 Vaccines:

1. Vaccines affect fertility.

There is no evidence that vaccines cause fertility problems in women or men.

2. Vaccines trigger chronic diseases and allergies.

Scientific studies have shown that vaccines do not cause chronic diseases and allergies.

3. Vaccines do not alleviate the spread of COVID-19.

It is widely proved that vaccines can contain the spread of COVID-19 and at least alleviate the severe symptoms.

4. The side effects of vaccines are hidden.

Most adverse reactions are short-lived and not serious, such as fever and mild pain around the point of injection. Only in rare cases would there be life-threatening adverse effects.

Misinformation about vaccines is almost everywhere, especially on social media. It is up to us to decide what to believe and what not to. If anyone is not sure about the information of COVID-19, it is always a good idea to consult a doctor about vaccine issues.

1. What is the topic of this report?

(A) Fake news is everywhere.

(B) Vaccines and your health.

(C) Some fake news about COVID-19 vaccines.

(D) The development of vaccines.

2. According to this article, what is NOT caused by COVID-19 vaccines?

(A) Infertility.

(B) Economic loss.

(C) Fever.

(D) Mild pain.

3. The word "trigger" of the first line of the 2. point is probably closest in meaning to?

(A) Influence.

(B) Cause.

(C) Happen.

(D) Originate.

4. **What is true about the side effects of COVID-19 vaccines?**

(A) There are no side effects.

(B) Pain-killers can prevent side effects.

(C) It is not worth getting vaccines because of the side effects.

(D) Some might feel feverish.

5. **In conclusion, what is suggested to do if you have questions about COVID-19 vaccines?**

(A) Discuss them with medical specialists.

(B) Look them up online.

(C) Do not take vaccines.

(D) Wait until others have taken vaccines.

關於新冠肺炎疫苗的假消息：

(1) 疫苗影響生育能力

沒有任何證據顯示疫苗引發女性或男性生育問題。

(2) 疫苗引發慢性疾病和過敏

科學研究顯示疫苗不會引起慢性疾病和過敏。

(3) 疫苗不會減緩新冠肺炎的擴散

疫苗能夠控制新冠肺炎的擴散，而且至少能夠減輕嚴重的症狀，這一點是經過廣泛證明的。

(4) 疫苗的副作用沒有公開

大部分的副作用是短暫的，而且不嚴重，例如發燒、注射處輕微的疼痛，只有少數個案會出現威脅生命的副作用。

關於疫苗的假消息幾乎到處可見，特別是在社群媒體，我們要決定什麼可信什麼不可信，如果有人對於新冠肺炎的資訊有不了解之處，最好的辦法就是向醫師諮詢相關事項。

1. 這篇報導的主題是什麼？

(A) 假消息到處都有。

(B) 疫苗與你的健康。

(C) 關於新冠肺炎的一些假消息。

(D) 疫苗的研發。

2. 根據這篇文章，何者不是由新冠肺炎所引起的？

(A) 不孕症。

(B) 經濟損失。

(C) 發燒。

(D) 輕微疼痛。

3. 第 (2) 點第一行的 "trigger" 意思最接近下列何者？

(A) 影響。

(B) 造成。

(C) 發生。

(D) 源自於。

4. 新冠肺炎疫苗的副作用何者為真？

(A) 沒有副作用。

(B) 止痛藥可以預防副作用。

(C) 因為副作用所以疫苗不值得打。

(D) 有些人有發燒症狀。

5. 總而言之，如果你有關於新冠肺炎的問題，你該怎麼做？

(A) 與醫學專家討論。

(B) 在網路上查詢。

(C) 不要打疫苗。

(D) 等別人打完疫苗。

Questions 11～15 refer to the following business e-mail.

(3)

To: Jennifer Baker

From: Debbie Ma

Date: Sep. 28, 2022

Subject: Registration for the Webinar for
Female Executives

Dear Ms. Baker,

It was nice meeting you at the trade fair in Taipei recently. You mentioned that you were going to host a forum held online solely for female executives early next month. I was wondering if there is still an opening for me. As I told you, I am not very familiar with the latest digital development as far as teleconferencing is concerned. Would it be possible if this time I could only be a listener, without making a presentation? Next time, I will certainly be able to contribute to the webinar after the first observing experience.

Please kindly reply regarding my application as a guest as soon as possible. I look forward to seeing you again and thank you very much.

Best Regards,

Debbie Ma
Debbie Bubble Tea
No. 7 Yongkang St
Taipei, Taiwan

1. What is the purpose of this e-mail?

(A) To become a volunteer online.

(B) To apply for a position online.

(C) To purchase a product online.

(D) To inquire about an online event.

2. What is most likely to be Debbie Ma's position?

(A) Secretary.

(B) Executive.

(C) Accountant.

(D) Sales assistant.

3. What does the writer of this e-mail prefer NOT to do in the online event?

(A) Coordinating the event.

(B) Donating money.

(C) Making a speech.

(D) Selling a product.

4. What is the closest meaning of "contribute" in the second last line of the first paragraph?

   (A) Donate.

   (B) Observe.

   (C) Write.

   (D) Give.

5. **What does Ms. Ma want Ms. Baker to inform her
   in the end of this e-mail?**

   (A) If she can take part in the event.

   (B) When the webinar will take place.

   (C) What she should do to participate the event.

   (D) If she has to do a report.

收信人：珍妮佛貝克
寄信人：馬黛比
日期：2022 年 9 月 28 日
主題：報名女性主管網路論壇

貝克女士　您好：

　　很高興不久前在台北商展上認識您，您提到將會於下個月初主辦一個專門邀請女性主管參加的網路論壇，我想知道是否還有一個名額讓我參加，如同我曾告訴您的，我對於關於遠距會議的最新數位發展，不是非常熟悉，是否可以這次我只是當觀眾而不發表簡報？有了第一次的旁聽經驗，下一次我一定會能夠對論壇做出貢獻。

　　請儘早回覆我這個旁聽申請是否可行，期待再次見到您，非常感謝。

順頌商祺

馬黛比
黛比珍珠奶茶
永康街 7 號
台北 台灣

1. 這封電子郵件的目的為何？

    (A) 為了當網路志工。

    (B) 為了申請一個網路上的職位。

    (C) 為了購買一個網路上的產品。

    (D) 為了詢問一個網路上的活動。

2. 馬黛比的職位最可能為何？

    (A) 秘書。

    (B) 主管。

    (C) 會計。

    (D) 業務助理。

3. 寫這封信的人在這個線上活動不想要做什麼？

    (A) 協調活動。

    (B) 捐錢。

    (C) 發表演說。

    (D) 銷售產品。

4. 第一段倒數第二行的 "**contribute**" 意思最接近什麼？

(A) 捐獻。

(B) 觀察。

(C) 寫作。

(D) 給予。

5. 在信尾馬女士希望貝克女士通知她什麼？

(A) 她是否能參加這個活動。

(B) 這個論壇何時舉行。

(C) 她要如何做才能參加這個活動。

(D) 她是否要做份報告。

Questions 16～20 refer to the following survey.

(4)

Kelly Supermarket

Customer Satisfaction Survey

B 1. **How long have you been shopping at Kelly Super market?**

(A) More than 2 years.

(B) 1～2 years.

(C) 6 months～1 year.

(D) Less than 6 months.

D 2. **How often do you shop at Kelly Supermarket?**

(A) More than 10 times a month.

(B) 7～9 times a month.

(C) 4～6 times a month.

(D) Less than 3 times a month.

3. **How do you rate the following features of Kelly Supermarket? (Please tick √)**

	Poor	Okay	Good	Very good
Prices of products		√		
Quality of products		√		
Variety of products			√	
Customer Service	√			

4. **Would you recommend your friends to shop at Kelly Supermarket? If no, why not?**

No, the service clerks are very impatient and rude.

5. **What suggestions do you have to make your shopping at Kelly Supermarket easier and more enjoyable?**

The service clerks should be trained in politeness.

1. What is the purpose of this survey?

(A) To see if the customers are pleased with the super-market.

(B) To see when the customers will come back to the supermarket.

(C) To see if the products are reasonably priced.

(D) To see what products the supermarket should sell.

2. What is NOT asked in this survey?

(A) The quality of the products.

(B) The quantity of the products.

(C) Opening hours of the supermarket.

(D) The customer service.

3. Why would the customer not recommend the super market to others?

(A) The service is inefficient.

(B) The service clerks' bad attitude.

(C) The products are too expensive.

(D) The quality of products is low.

4. What does the customer think the service clerks should work on?

(A) Knowledge of the products.

(B) Speed of serving customers

(C) Politeness and manners.

(D) Packaging the products.

凱莉超市

客戶滿意度調查

B **1.** 您在凱莉超市購物有多久了？

(A) 超過兩年。

(B) 1 至 2 年。

(C) 6 個月至 1 年。

(D) 少於 6 個月。

D **2.** 您多常在凱莉超市購物？

(A) 1 個月超過 10 次。

(B) 1 個月 7～9 次。

(C) 1 個月 4～6 次。

(D) 1 個月少於 3 次。

3. 您對於凱莉超市下列項目的評價如何？（請打勾 √）

	差	尚可	良好	非常好
產品價格		√		
產品品質		√		
產品多元程度			√	
客戶服務	√			

4. 您會推薦您的朋友來凱莉超市購物嗎？如果不會，是什麼原因呢？

<u>不會，客服人員非常沒耐心且沒禮貌。</u>

5. 您有什麼建議能讓凱莉購物更容易且更有意思？

<u>客服人員應該接受禮貌訓練。</u>

1. 這調查的目的為何？

(A) 為了要看顧客是否對此超市滿意。

(B) 為了要看顧客是否會回來光顧。

(C) 為了要看產品是否標價合理。

(D) 為了要看超市該賣什麼產品。

2. 這調查裡沒有問到什麼？

(A) 產品的品質。

(B) 產品的數量。

(C) 此超市的營業時間。

(D) 顧客服務。

3. 這個顧客為什麼不會推薦此超市給別人？

(A) 服務沒效率。

(B) 客服人員態度差。

(C) 產品太貴。

(D) 產品品質差。

4. 這位顧客認為客服人員應加強什麼？

(A) 產品知識。

(B) 服務客戶的速度。

(C) 禮貌和禮儀。

(D) 產品包裝。

Questions 20～24 refer to the following board meeting minutes.

(5)

James Wang Architecture Firm

Board Meeting Minutes: Sep. 29, 2021
No. 100, Tunhua N. Rd, Taipei

Board Attendees: James Wang, Mai Lin, Ted Jiang, Henry Chung, Kevin Li, Doris Han, Lucy Wen, Mingde Perng
Absentees: Kelly Wang
Guests: Jenny Lai, Larry Ho

Minutes presented by: Jessica Li

Call to order
9:00 a.m. By Mr. James Wang

Orders of Business
Reports
CEO's Report, Mr. James Wang
First Mr. James Wang introduced new hires, new assistant Jenny Lai and new accountant Larry. Then Mr.

James Wang announced that the company won the Award of Best Green Architecture on Campus, and he emphasized the objectives of the company. Then followed the discussion.

Financial Director's Report, Mr. Mai Lin

The Award of Best Green Architecture on Campus brought in 1000,000 Taiwan Dollars. The new cleaning service saves the company 10,000 Taiwan Dollars per month. The company is in the process of finalizing the contract with a new building material supplier, which can save substantial budgets.

Sales Manager's Report, Mr. Ted Jiang

Last week the sales team participated an online fair of Green Architecture and conducted a sales campaign with representatives from various countries.

Unfinished business

Due to the pandemic, the renovation of Lin Residence in Wanghua was delayed and should be carried on immediately.

New business

New project of the green Library will soon be com-menced.

Closing

Meeting adjourned at: 11:30 am, Sep. 29, 2021

Next meeting date: Dec 10, 2021

1. What is this statement most likely to be written for?

(A) To report to the press.

(B) To apply for a government grant.

(C) To announce the company shares.

(D) To record a formal meeting.

2. Who is the person that calls for the meeting?

(A) The CEO.

(B) The financial director.

(C) Ms. Kelly Wang.

(D) The Sales manager

3. What is NOT stated in the report of the financial director?

(A) A fair of green architecture.

(B) An award prize of architecture.

(C) A new cleaning company.

(D) A new company of building materials.

4. What causes the delay of the project of Lin Residence in Wanghua?

(A) The seasonal flu.

(B) The outbreak of COVID-19.

(C) The shortage of building materials.

(D) The family disputes.

5. What does "adjourn" in the last second line closest in meaning to?

(A) Put down.

(B) Put away.

(C) Put out.

(D) Put off.

王建名建築師事務所

董事會議紀錄：2021 年 9 月 29 日
台北市敦化北路 100 號

董事會議與會者：王建名、林邁、江泰德、鍾恆利、
李凱文、韓朵莉、文露西、彭明德
缺席者：王凱莉
客人：賴珍妮、何賴利
會議記錄者：李潔西卡
宣布開會
王建名上午 9 點宣布開會
議程
報告
執行長報告，王建名先生
首先王建名先生介紹新進人員：新助理賴珍妮、新
會計何賴利，然後宣布公司得到了最佳校園綠建築
獎，並且強調了公司目標，之後展開討論。
財務主任報告，林邁先生
最佳校園綠建築獎為公司進帳 100 萬台幣，新清潔公
司為公司每月省了一萬元，公司正在與一家新建材
公司擬定合約，可以省下大量經費。

業務經理報告，江泰德先生

上星期銷售團隊參加綠建築線上商展，而且與不同國家代表進行了銷售宣傳活動。

未完成事項

因為疫情，萬華林宅整修進度延後，必須馬上繼續進行。

新事項

綠圖書館的新建案很快就會開始。

尾聲

2021 年 9 月 29 日上午 11:30 休會。

下次會議日期：2021 年 12 月 10 日

1. 這篇文章最可能是為何而寫？

   (A) 向媒體報告。

   (B) 申請政府補助。

   (C) 宣布公司股份。

   (D) 紀錄一場正式會議。

2. 是誰召開會議的？

   (A) 執行長。

   (B) 財務主任。

   (C) 王凱莉女士。

   (D) 業務經理。

3. 財務主任的報告內沒有包括什麼？

   (A) 一個綠建築商展。

   (B) 建築獎項的獎金。

   (C) 一個新清潔公司。

   (D) 一個新建材公司。

4. 是什麼造成萬華林宅專案的延誤？

(A) 季節流感。

(B) 新冠肺炎爆發。

(C) 建材短缺。

(D) 家族紛爭。

5. 倒數第二行的 "**adjourn**" 最接近什麼意思？

(A) 放下。

(B) 收拾。

(C) 熄滅。

(D) 休會。

Questions 25-29 refer to the following report.

(6)

The Tokyo Summer Olympics Opening Ceremony successfully took place yesterday

Athletes and viewers waited almost exact one year for the Tokyo Summer Olympics to take place due to the pandemic. Yesterday the grand Olympics Opening Ceremony were watched worldwide on various media. It was staged in the New National Stadium, designed by Mr. Kengo Kuma, a renowned Japanese architect. The stadium features a wooden lattice design resembling traditional Japanese shrines. Its specially-designed wood-and-steel roof is made partially of Japanese cedar trees and can open in the center to transform the original stadium into an open-air stadium. The architect intends with this design to relink the Tokyo city with the nature. As Tokyo declared Coronavirus state of emergency recently, general spectators were not allowed in the ceremony. Only a group of diplomats, foreign dig-nitaries, Olympic sponsors and members of the International Olympic Committee were in attendance of the ceremony. All in all, it exhibited a unique and excellent athlete and artistic components of the culture of Japan. The viewers of world experienced a well-executed program in the ceremony, showing successfully host country's national identity on a global stage, which is the main purpose of the Olympics Opening Ceremony.

1. Why was the Tokyo Summer Olympics postponed?

(A) Due to the vaccinations.

(B) Due to the earthquakes.

(C) Due to the outbreak of COVID-19.

(D) Due to the corruptions.

2. What is in the concept of the famous architect Kengo Kuma in designing the stadium?

(A) To restore the patriotism of Japanese.

(B) To restore the link Tokyo's loss with nature.

(C) To restore the trust with the committee.

(D) To restore the ancient buildings.

3. **Who was NOT present in the Opening Ceremony?**

(A) Olympic sponsors.

(B) Foreign dignitaries

(C) Diplomats

(D) General spectators.

4. **What is the closest meaning of "on a global stage" in the last sentence?**

(A) in the theater.

(B) in the stadium.

(C) in the Internet.

(D) in the world.

5. **What is the main objective of having the Olympics Opening Ceremony?**

(A) Showing off the wealth of the host nation.

(B) Showing the national identity of the host country.

(C) Showing the efforts of the Olympics committee.

(D) Showing the importance of the stadium.

東京夏季奧運開幕式昨天順利舉行

因為疫情，運動員和觀眾等了近一年才盼到東京奧運會順利舉行，昨天全世界觀眾在各媒體都觀賞了奧運盛大開幕典禮，典禮是在新國家運動場舉行，此運動場是由日本知名建築師隈研吾先生所設計，特徵為木造格子花樣，形似傳統日本神社，特殊木材與鋼筋合成屋頂，部分採用日本雪松，可由中間打開將原有運動場變為露天運動場，藉此設計連結東京都與大自然。因為東京發布新冠肺炎緊急事態宣言，一般觀眾無法參加開幕典禮，只有一些外交官、外國親貴、奧運贊助者、國際奧運委員會成員能參加觀禮。總而言之，典禮展示了日本文化獨特的運動與藝術特色，讓世界觀眾充分欣賞到傑出的表演節目，於國際舞台上成功展示了主辦國的國家特色，這就是奧運開幕典禮的主要目的。

1. 東京夏季奧運為何延辦？

   (A) 因為疫苗。

   (B) 因為地震。

   (C) 因為新冠肺炎爆發。

   (D) 因為賄賂。

2. 知名建築師隈研吾先生設計這個運動場的概念為何？

   (A) 重建日本愛國精神。

   (B) 重建東京與自然的連結。

   (C) 重建與委員會的信任。

   (D) 重建古建築。

3. 誰沒有出席這個開幕式？

   (A) 奧運贊助者。

   (B) 外國親貴。

   (C) 外交官。

   (D) 一般觀賽者。

4. 最後一句中的 **"on a global stage"** 最接近什麼意思？

   (A) 在劇院。

   (B) 在運動場。

   (C) 在網路上。

   (D) 在世界上。

5. 奧運開幕典禮的主要目的為何？

   (A) 炫耀主辦國的財力。

   (B) 展示主辦國的國家特色。

   (C) 展示奧運委員會的努力。

   (D) 展示運動場的重要性。

兩篇

Questions XXX—XXX refer to the following book review and e-mail.

(1)

Monthly review

Eun-sook Kim shares for the first time in her newly released book "From the North" her own experiences of early life in North Korea, where she escaped from as a teenager. In her autobiographical writing, she reveals how it was like, as an undocumented immigrant, working on the assembly line in a factory in the UK. What's more, her experiences of working as a waitress illegally and teaching herself English and in the 90s, while hiding from the immigration officers. She is now a self-taught author.

"From the North" is her first book and already a bestseller in many English-speaking countries. The edition of complicated Chinese was just released last week in Taiwan.

From: Judy Yang

To: Eun-sook Kim

Date: Oct. 4, 2022

Subject: Speech invitation

Dear Ms. Kim,

Congratulations for the success of your debut book: "From the North" . With the recent release of the edition of complicated Chinese in Taiwan, we would like to invite you to visit our high school to share your stories with the students. Of course, you can share whatever you would like to talk about with our students as well, such as writing and travel. We will organize a book-signing event in the end of your speech and Q&A session. Please let us know if this suits the schedule in your book tour in Asia and how you would like us accommodate the whole event. Thank you very much and we look forward to your visit.

Warm Regards,

Judy Yang

Head of school

1. What is the monthly review about?

(A) The best new books of the library.

(B) The report of a new bestseller.

(C) The hard work of translation.

(D) The illegal immigration.

2. What is the purpose of this e-mail?

(A) To discuss the copyright.

(B) To set up an interview.

(C) To invite a writer to visit a school.

(D) To ask an author to make a video talk.

3. According to the review, what makes the author so special?

(A) She shares her personal experiences of escaping from North Korea.

(B) She shares in the book the secrets of realizing American Dream.

(C) She reveals in the book the family saga of the leader of North Korea.

(D) She reveals the secrets of early Korean immigrants to the US.

4. According to the e-mail, why is it a good timing for the writer to visit the high school now?

(A) The author just came back from South Korea.

(B) The history class at the high school just covered North Korea.

(C) The edition of complicated Chinese was recently released.

(D) The author feels like traveling around the world.

5. What will be included in the end of the speech to the high school?

(A) Book-signing event.

(B) Special exhibition of North Korea.

(C) Lucky draw of tickets to North Korea.

(D) Guided tour in the city.

每月書評

　　金銀淑在她的新書《來自北方》中第一次分享她早年在北韓的生活經驗，也就是她青少年時期逃離之處，在她的自傳裡，她透露了在英國工廠生產線上當非法移工的真實生活，還有她在 90 年代當非法服務生並且自學英文的過去，那時她還得要躲避移民署查緝。現在她是一位自學而成的作家，《來自北方》是她的第一本書，於很多英語系國家已經成為暢銷書，中文繁體字版本上星期剛剛在台灣上市。

　　寄件人：楊茱蒂
　　收件人：金銀淑
　　日期：2022 年 10 月 4 日
　　主旨：演講邀請

　　金女士您好

　　恭喜您首部作品《來自北方》順利問世，最近繁體字版本剛於台發行，我們想要邀請您來我們高中與學生分享您的故事，當然您也可以分享任何您想要與我們學生討論的事情，例如寫作與旅行。我們將會在您演講與提問時間完畢後安排一個簽書會，請讓我們知道您亞洲新書宣傳活動中是否安排進去這個行程，以及我們該如何準備這整個活動。非常感謝您也期待您的來訪。

順頌時綏

楊茱蒂

校長

1. 這篇每月評論內容主要是關於什麼？

(A) 圖書館中最佳新書。

(B) 一本新暢銷書的報導。

(C) 翻譯的辛苦工作。

(D) 非法移民。

2. 這封電子郵件的目的為何？

(A) 討論版權。

(B) 安排面談。

(C) 邀請一位作者到學校參訪。

(D) 請一位作者做視訊談話。

3. 根據這個評論，什麼是作者最特別的地方？

(A) 她分享個人逃離北韓的經驗。

(B) 她分享實現美國夢的秘訣。

(C) 她揭露了北韓領導人的家族秘辛。

(D) 她揭露了早期韓國移民到美國的秘密。

4. 根據這封電子郵件，為什麼現在是這位作者參訪高中的好時機？

(A) 這位作者剛從北韓回來。

(B) 這所高中的歷史課剛好上到北韓。

(C) 繁體字版本剛於台發行。

(D) 這位作者想要環遊世界。

5. 在高中演講結束後會有什麼活動？

(A) 簽書會。

(B) 北韓特展。

(C) 北韓機票抽獎。

(D) 該城市導覽。

兩篇

(2)

Uncle Sam English

"Uncle Sam English" has enjoyed an excellent reputation of English teaching and is a pioneer in offering online courses. In addition to face-to-face classes, the online courses are offered as well. Both are conducted in group classes and in one-on-one sessions by well-qualified teachers.

Currently, we offer the following courses:

(1) Basic course

(2) Grammar course

(3) Conversation course

(4) Business Communication course

(5) TOEIC preparation course

If you are not sure which course suits you, we strongly suggest you to book a free placement test online in advance with us. After the assessment, one of our teachers will have a discussion with you as to which level you are and which course you should take.

From: James Chen
To: Sam Smith
Date: Oct. 5, 2022
Subject: Inquiries of English courses

Dear Sir/Madam,

Some of my colleagues recommended your language school to me. I'd like to know if you offer TOEIC preparation course because recently my supervisor asked me to take the TOEIC test. In order to gain a higher position, I decide to take time to prepare for the test. My English is about a high school graduate's level, and I definitely have to learn grammar all over again. The online placement test seems just what I need right now. Please schedule it for me as soon as possible. Ideally, I would like to take both in-person and online classes. It depends much on the fees regarding whether I should take individual or small group classes. I wouldn't mind learning with a small team of students if we are on the similar level of English. Thank you.

Best Regards,
James Chen
Sales Manager
Dachen Pharmaceutical Co., Ltd.

1. **What is the first passage mainly about?**

   (A) To promote language learning books.

   (B) To advertise English courses.

   (C) To describe a newly opened school.

   (D) To sell learning aids online.

2. **What is placement test possibly for?**

   (A) To send students to other places.

   (B) To help students get ideal positions.

   (C) To place students in the right levels.

   (D) To separate students to several small groups.

3. **What makes the man want to choose this language school?**

   (A) He thinks the fees are reasonable.

   (B) He has taken courses from the school before.

   (C) He knows some good teachers from the school.

   (D) He heard many good things about the school from his colleagues.

4. **Why does the man want to take TOEIC preparation course?**

(A) To meet the requirement of his company.

(B) To be able to host visitors from abroad.

(C) To take business trips overseas.

(D) To become an international businessman.

5. **What is the man's main concern about choosing one-on-one or small group classes?**

(A) The other students.

(B) The class hours.

(C) The teachers.

(D) The tuition.

山姆大叔英文

　　山姆大叔英文在英語教學界享有優良聲譽，領先業界創先提供線上課程，除了面對面實體課程外，同時也提供線上課程，兩者皆有小班制團體和個人班課程，都由優良合格老師指導。

　　目前我們提供以下課程：

(1) 基礎課程

(2) 文法課程

(3) 會話課程

(4) 商業會談課程

(5) 多益準備課程

　　如果您不太確定哪個課程適合您，我們強烈建議您與我們預約線上分級測驗，經過評估後，我們會請一位老師與您討論您的程度以及適合您的課程。

寄件人：陳健明
收件人：山姆史密斯
日期：2022 年 10 月 5 日
主旨：詢問英文課程

您好：

　　有同事向我推薦貴語言學校，我想要知道貴校是否有提供多益準備課程，因為我的上司要求我參加多益考試，為了要獲得升遷，我決定要挪出時間來準備這個考試，我的英文程度大概是高中畢業生的程度，我一定得要重學文法。線上分級測驗似乎正是我目前所需要的，請幫我儘快安排，理想狀態下我想要實體與線上課程同時進行，至於我該選個人課程或小班制團體課程，這主要看學費而定，如果程度相近的話，我可以接受上小班制團體。謝謝您。

敬祝教安

陳健明
業務經理

大成藥品有限公司

1. 第一篇文章的主旨為何？

(A) 促銷語言學習書籍。

(B) 廣告英文課程。

(C) 描述一家新開的學校。

(D) 於網路上賣教具。

2. 分級測驗的目的可能為何？

(A) 將學生送到其它地方。

(B) 幫助學生到達理想地方。

(C) 將學生分到適合程度。

(D) 將學生分成幾個小組。

3. 這個男子為什麼想要選擇這家語言學校？

(A) 他覺得學費合理。

(B) 他之前曾經在這間學校修過課。

(C) 他知道這間學校的一些老師很好。

(D) 他從同事那裡聽到很多關於這間學校的好評。

4. 為什麼這個男子想要學習多益準備課程？

(A) 以符合他公司的需求。

(B) 以接待外國來的訪客。

(C) 以到外國出差。

(D) 以成為國際企業人士。

5. 關於選擇一對一或是小班制團體，這個男子主要的考量是什麼？

(A) 其他學生。

(B) 上課時數。

(C) 教師。

(D) 學費。

兩篇

(3)

Questions XXX—XXX refer to the following report and messenger exchanges.

2021/10/04

The easing of restrictions for dining-in in restaurants.

TAIPEI (Taiwan News) — The Taiwan Central Epidemic Command Center (CECC) on Monday (Oct. 4) announced that it will loosen epidemic prevention regulations for restaurants starting Tuesday (Oct. 5) . CECC Spokesperson Chuang Jen-hsiang said the local outbreak remains under control despite large crowds during Mid-Autumn Festival two weeks ago.

Starting on Oct. 5, restaurants will no longer need partitions on tables or have to enforce social distancing of 1.5 meters, while toasting tables with alcohol will again be allowed. Diners must wear masks when leaving their table and toasting guests at other tables. The key point is that you are expressing gratitude with gestures of toasting, not drinking the wine. The rules on the serving of dishes at tables and in buffet lines will also be relaxed, with specific staff members no longer required to serve buffet customers dishes or allocate portions. Name registration will continue to be conducted at all restaurants for contact tracing.

Messengers

Anna

Have you heard starting from today, the epidemic prevention regulations will be eased?

Bob

No, like what?

Anna

Like indoor dining without partitions. No need for checkerboard seating.

Bob

Really? Do you think that would be safe?

Anna

Hard to tell. I'd probably prefer takeouts.

Bob

Maybe I'll start with a restaurant with outdoor seats.

Anna

> The problem is that outdoor seats are often occupied by smokers.

Bob

> That's really annoying.

Anna

> At the moment, let's have picnic with takeouts during lunch breaks in the park nearby.

Bob

> I totally agree.

1. **What is the general topic in the above passages?**

   (A) The regulations for restaurants will be eased.

   (B) No more reservation in advance is needed.

   (C) It is still banned to toast guests in restaurants.

   (D) Dining-in is still not allowed in restaurants.

2. **Why is all restaurants required to conduct name registration?**

   (A) To count the number of customers.

   (B) To trace the contacts of COVID-19 patients.

   (C) To reduce the contacts of confirmed cases.

   (D) To apply for subsidies from the government.

3. **What does Anna mean by saying "Hard to tell." ?**

   (A) She is not sure.

   (B) She does not like the idea.

   (C) She will not go to a restaurant.

   (D) She disagrees with the rule.

4. What does Bob find it annoying?

(A) The seats are not enough for all guests.

(B) Bob prefers taking his own food by himself in a buffet restaurant.

(C) The air is polluted by cigarette smoke.

(D) Anna smokes too much after a meal.

5. What do A and B agree in the end of their con versation?

(A) Dining in a restaurant.

(B) Taking a break at noon.

(C) Having their lunch in a park.

(D) Ordering food delivery for lunch.

餐廳解除內用限制

　　台北（台灣英文新聞）— 中央疫情指揮中心於10月4日星期一宣布將於10月5日星期二鬆綁餐廳防疫措施，指揮中心發言人莊人祥說雖然兩星期前中秋節假期間有群眾現象，地方疫情仍維持穩定控制狀態。

　　10月5日起，餐廳桌上不再需要隔板，也不需要保持社交距離1.5公尺，餐桌敬酒也不再禁止，離開自己餐桌到他人餐桌敬酒必須要戴口罩，重點是用敬酒的姿態表達感謝，而不是喝酒。關於餐桌與自助餐的規定也鬆綁，不再需要服務員來幫忙夾菜。所有的餐廳仍然必須要實行實名制，以追蹤確診足跡。

Messengers

安娜

你聽說了嗎？從今天起，防疫規定會鬆綁？

鮑伯

沒有呢，像什麼呢？

安娜

像是內用不需要隔板，也不需要梅花座。

鮑伯

真的嗎？妳認為那樣安全嗎？

安娜

很難說，我還是比較喜歡外帶。

鮑伯

或許我會先從有戶外座位的餐廳開始。

安娜

問題是戶外座位常常坐滿吸菸的人

鮑伯

真是煩人啊。

安娜

現在，我們午餐時間還是買外帶到附近公園午餐吧。

鮑伯

我舉雙手贊成！

1. 以上文字的主要大意為何？

    (A) 餐廳規定將會鬆綁。

    (B) 不需要事先預約。

    (C) 在餐廳仍然禁止敬酒

    (D) 在餐廳仍然禁止內用。

2. 為何所有餐廳必須實行實名制？

    (A) 為了計數顧客人數。

    (B) 為了追蹤新冠肺炎患者的足跡。

    (C) 為了減少確診者的接觸。

    (D) 為了申請政府的補助。

3. 安娜說 "**Hard to tell.**" 是什麼意思？

    (A) 她不確定。

    (B) 她不喜歡這個主意。

    (C) 她不要去餐廳。

    (D) 她不同意這規定。

4. 鮑伯覺得什麼很煩人？

(A) 座位不夠所有客人坐。

(B) 鮑伯比較喜歡自己夾自助餐的餐點。

(C) 空氣被菸味汙染。

(D) 安娜在餐後抽太多菸。

5. 談話結尾時安娜和鮑伯最後同意做什麼？

(A) 在餐廳吃飯。

(B) 中午休息一下。

(C) 在公園吃午餐。

(D) 午餐叫外送。

三篇

(4)

Questions XXX—XXX refer to the following report, advertisement and e-mail.

2021/09/07

COVID-19 Outbreaks in kindergarten and schools in New Taipei City

TAIPEI (Taiwan News) — On Sunday (Sept. 5), New Taipei Mayor Hou You-yi announced that a man and his wife tested positive for COVID-19. The next day, Mayor Hou reported nine cases tied to a kindergarten where the woman works as a teacher. By Tuesday morning (Sept. 7), five more students and parents had been diagnosed with the disease, bringing the total number of cases tied to a cluster infection at the kindergarten to 15. Cases have started to crop up at other schools across New Taipei City, with two elementary schools announcing closures and three canceling specific classes. Thus far, 4300 students have been sent home as a result of the closures.

Wonder Nanny

Feeling exhausted by your children during this hard time? Unable to do remote working while attending to your small kids at home? We have the solution for you: Wonder Nannies! In our database you can find certified babysitters, who can take care of your kids at your residence or your designated places. We understand you might just need a nanny for the time being, so there is no need to sign a long-term contract. Our nannies specialize in providing respite care service for pre-school children. Don't hesitate to give us a call and tell us your needs for child care.

Mandy Chen
Mandy Child Care

From: Jerry Chu
To: Mandy Chen
Date: Oct. 5, 2021
Subject: Inquiries of babysitting service

Dear Ms. Mandy Chen,

I saw the advertisement of your child care service on the bulletin board of the kindergarten of my two small kids. Currently due to the outbreak of COVID-19, my 5-year boy and 4-year girl cannot attend the kindergarten. As a single father, I desperately need a nanny to look after my kids at my place while I work during daytime. Please arrange an English-speaking nanny for us because my kids spent their early years in the US and can understand English much better than Chinese. Your prompt reply will be much appreciated.

Best Regards,

Jerry Chu

1. What is the news report mainly about?

(A) The death numbers of COVID-19 cases.

(B) The outbreak of COVID-19 in a kindergarten.

(C) The market for caregivers.

(D) The importance of vaccination for kids.

2. What is the general tone of the news report?

(A) Cautious.

(B) Playful.

(C) Humorous.

(D) Relaxing.

3. What service does the company advertise for?

(A) Private English tutoring.

(B) Babysitting for small children.

(C) Helpers for housework.

(D) Care for people with disabilities

4. **What is the closest meaning of the phrase "respite care service" here?**

   (A) Care for senior citizens.

   (B) Short-term holidays.

   (C) Supplemental services.

   (D) Long-term support.

5. **Why does the man in his e-mail request for an English-speaking nanny?**

   (A) His children grew up in the US.

   (B) He does not want a Chinese-speaking nanny.

   (C) He cannot speak Chinese very well.

   (D) His children are learning English.

2021/09/07

新北市幼兒園和學校爆發新冠肺炎

台北（台灣英文新聞）－ 新北市長侯友宜在 9 月 5 日星期日宣布一名男子和他的太太確診新冠肺炎，第二天，這位太太教書的幼兒園爆發了 9 個個案，到了 9 月 7 日星期二早上，又多了 5 名學生和家長確診，幼兒園群聚感染總數來到了 15 人，新北市內其他學校確診案例如雨後春筍般爆發，兩間小學宣布停課，三間取消特定課程，到目前為止，已經有 4300 學生因為停課而被遣送回家。

神奇保姆

在這個艱困的時刻因為要照顧您的小孩感到筋疲力盡嗎？無法在家一邊照顧小小孩一邊居家工作嗎？我們有解決辦法提供給您：神奇保姆！在我們的資料庫中，您可以找到合格的保姆，可以到府上或是到您指定地點照顧您的小孩。我們了解您可能只是短時間需要保姆，所以不需要您簽長期合約，我們公司特別擅長照顧學齡前兒童的喘息服務。不要猶豫，馬上打電話給我們，告訴我們您的保姆需求。

陳曼蒂
曼蒂保姆

From: 朱傑瑞
To: 陳曼蒂
Date: 2021 年 10 月 5 日
Subject: 詢問保姆服務

陳曼蒂女士您好：

　　我看見您在我兩個小小孩的幼兒園布告欄所貼的保姆廣告，現在因為新冠肺炎爆發，我的五歲兒了和四歲女兒無法去幼兒園上課，身為單身父親，我急需一位保姆在我白天工作時，來我家照顧我的小孩。請為我們安排一位會說英語的保姆，因為我的小孩在美國出生長大，對英文的理解比中文好很多。希望能儘早回覆，非常感謝您。

　　順頌時綏
　　朱傑瑞

1. 這篇新聞報導主要是關於什麼主題？

(A) 新冠肺炎的死亡人數。

(B) 幼兒園爆發新冠肺炎。

(C) 看護的市場。

(D) 小孩施打疫苗的重要性。

2. 這篇新聞報導的口吻大致是怎麼樣的？

(A) 謹慎的。

(B) 開玩笑的。

(C) 幽默的。

(D) 放鬆的。

3. 這家公司廣告什麼服務？

(A) 私人英文家教。

(B) 小小孩保母服務。

(C) 家事幫手。

(D) 身心障礙人士的看護。

4. 這裡的 "**respite care service**" 最接近下列何意？

(A) 銀髮族的照護。

(B) 短期的假期。

(C) 追加的服務。

(D) 長期的支持。

5. 為什麼這個男子在他的電子郵件中要求要一個説英語的保母？

(A) 他的小孩在美國長大。

(B) 他不要說中文的保母。

(C) 他無法說流利的中文。

(D) 他的小孩正在學英語。

三篇

(5)

Questions XXX—XXX refer to the following report and two e-mails.

Taipei
Oct 10, 2022

Facebook has a new issue that causes parents to concern. It is reported that quite a few teenagers easily acquired alcoholic products on the platform, especially beer. _____[1]_____ Although according to the current regulations, consumers can only purchase alcoholic products when they provide ID photos to prove they are above 18 years old. Nevertheless, companies posting alcohol advertisements on Facebook and other social media seem to be able to find ways to get around this rule. _____[2]_____ Officers of Consumers' Foundation urge the alcohol companies do not sell alcohol to teenagers, otherwise they will breach the Children and Youth Welfare Act.

From: Jenny Smith

To: Gold Beer

Date: Oct. 13, 2022

Subject: Selling alcohol to teenagers

Dear Sir/Madam,

Last Saturday, my 13-year-old son bought your beer online via the advertisement you posted on Facebook. Don't you know it is illegal to sell alcoholic products to people under 18 years old? _____[3]_____ Do take down the Ad posts on the Facebook immediately or I will take legal actions against your beer company.

Jenny Smith

From: John Li

To: Jenny Smith

Date: Oct 14, 2022

Subject: Re: Selling alcohol to teenagers

Dear Ms. Smith,

We are sorry things like this could happen with our company. We do require the ID photo of the buyer before we deliver the alcoholic products. I just checked the papers and found what your son provided was probably your ID photo. _____[4]_____ We apologize for not checking it thoroughly, and we will come up with a new way to prevent this from happening again.

Best Regards,

John Li

Manager,

Gold beer

1. **What is the general topic of the above passages?**

   (A) The importing of famous beer to Taiwan.

   (B) The negotiation of beer prices for teenagers.

   (C) The selling of alcoholic products to teenagers on Facebook.

   (D) The return of low-quality beer products via Facebook.

2. **Why does the mother of the teenager write the e-mail?**

   (A) She wants to complain about something.

   (B) She thinks her son is overcharged.

   (C) She finds out her son uses her credit card.

   (D) She has a new business idea.

3. **According to the manager's reply, what might be the reason the teenager got the beer?**

   (A) He worked for the beer company part-time.

   (B) He provided his mother's ID photo.

   (C) He used online payment.

   (D) He asked his father to buy the beer for him.

4. In which of the positions marked [1], [2], [3] and [4] does the following sentence best belong? "It is not only against the Children and Youth Welfare Act; it is also against common sense."

   (A) [1]

   (B) [2]

   (C) [3]

   (D) [4]

5. What in the end does the manager promised to do?

   (A) To deliver the beer in person.

   (B) To stop the misuse of false ID photo.

   (C) To hire more customer service clerks.

   (D) To offer discounts to the mother.

報導

台北

2022 年 10 月 10 日

脸書有一件令家長擔憂的新問題，據說不少的青少年可以輕易於此平台購得酒類產品，特別是啤酒。

_____[1]_____ 雖然根據現行法規，消費者只需要提供身份證照片，證明他們年滿 18 歲，才能購買酒精類產品，然而，於脸書與其它社群媒體刊登酒類廣告的公司，似乎能鑽法律漏洞，_____[2]_____ 消保官呼籲酒類公司不要賣酒給青少年，否則會觸犯兒童及少年福利與權益保障法。

From: 珍妮史密斯

To: 金啤酒

Date: 2022 年 10 月 13 日

Subject: 販賣酒類給未成年人

敬啟者：

　　上星期六我 13 歲兒子透過你們臉書上的廣告，網購了你們家啤酒。你們難道不知道販賣酒類給 18 歲以下未成年人是犯法的嗎？　　　[3]　　　請務必馬上將廣告由臉書卸下，否則我將會對貴公司採取法律行動。

　　珍妮史密斯

- -

From: 李約翰
To: 珍妮史密斯
Date: 2022 年 10 月 14 日
Subject: Re: 販賣酒類給未成年人

史密斯夫人　您好：

　　我們對於發生這樣的事情感到很遺憾，我們的確有
要求買家提供身份証照片，才販售酒類產品。剛才我查
了一下文件，發現貴公子提供的身份証照片可能是您的。
　　[4]　　　　我們對於沒有仔細檢查照片向您致歉，我
們會研擬新辦法來避免類似情形再度發生。

　　敬祝健康

　　李約翰
　　經理
　　金啤酒

1. 以上文字大致的主題為何？

(A) 進口有名的啤酒到台灣。

(B) 為青少年議價啤酒。

(C) 臉書上販賣酒類給未成年人。

(D) 透過臉書將劣質的啤酒產品退貨。

2. 為什麼這位青少年的母親要寫這封電子郵件？

(A) 她想要抱怨某件事。

(B) 她認為她的兒子被敲詐了。

(C) 她發現她的兒子用了她的信用卡。

(D) 她有了一個商業新點子。

3. 根據這位經理的回覆，這個青少年買到啤酒的原因可能為何？

(A) 他在此啤酒公司兼差

(B) 他提供了他母親的身份証照片。

(C) 他用了線上支付。

(D) 他要求他父親買啤酒給他。

4. 以下這一句話最適合放在 **[1], [2], [3], [4]** 中的哪一處？ "**It is not only against the Children and Youth Welfare Act; it is also against common sense.**"

(A) [1]

(B) [2]

(C) [3]

(D) [4]

5. 最後經理承諾要做什麼？

(A) 會親自送啤酒來。

(B) 會喝止不當使用假身份証照片。

(C) 會雇用更多的客服人員。

(D) 會提供這位母親折扣。

正確答案：

	1.	2.	3.	4.	5.
(1)	C	A	A	D	B
(2)	C	A	B	D	A
(3)	D	B	C	D	A
(4)	A	C	B	C	
(5)	D	A	A	B	D
(6)	C	B	D	D	B

	1.	2.	3.	4.	5.
(1)	B	C	A	C	A
(2)	B	C	D	A	D
(3)	A	B	A	C	C
(4)	B	A	B	C	A
(5)	C	A	B	C	B

後記

希望這本書能夠於多益閱讀中助你一臂之力，職場英文閱讀效率也能隨之大幅提升！

聽力&口說

★ ★ ★

The General English Proficiency Test | Intermedia
Listening Comprehension& Speaking

★ 素養導向評量，適合用來準備校內外各類英文考試！

★ 本書對所有想提昇英語程度的學習者皆適用！

★ 幫助您自修英語的聽力和口說能力！

★ 個人英語進修的實用學習工具書！

中級 新制全民英檢 GEPT
The General English Proficiency Test [Intermediate]
聽力&口說 模擬試題+解答
QR Code （附QR Code隨掃隨聽音檔）

雅典文化

準備GEPT全民英檢的實用工具書

完全掌握全民英檢中級聽力和口說能力的命題方向和題型
新題型依據108課綱，素養導向命題；實用英語，貼近日常生活，解決問題。

完整資訊：
提供所有關於全民英檢中級必知的Q&A。

準備要領：
分為平日培養英語閱讀和寫作能力的方法，以及針對閱讀和寫作能力測驗的準備要點。

模擬試題：
提供仿真模擬試題三回，並附上中文詳盡翻譯與解析。

必背520字：
提供出現頻率最高的520個單字，加上同義字，皆為日常生活常用的字彙，宜勤加背誦。

閱讀&寫作

★ ★ ★

The General English Proficiency Test [Intermediate]
Reading & Writing

★ 素養導向評量，適合用來準備校內外各類英文考試！

★ 本書對所有想提昇英語程度的學習者皆適用！

★ 幫助您自修英語的閱讀和寫作能力！

★ 個人英語進修的實用學習工具書！

中級 新制全民英檢 GEPT
The General English Proficiency Test [Intermediate]
閱讀&寫作 模擬試題+解答
 QR Code （附QR Code隨掃隨聽音檔）

雅典文化

準備GEPT全民英檢的實用工具書

完全掌握全民英檢中級閱讀和寫作能力的命題方向和題型
新題型依據108課綱，素養導向命題；實用英語，貼近日常生活，解決問題。

全民英檢中級的完整資訊：
提供所有關於全民英檢中級必知的Q&A。

閱讀和寫作能力的準備要領：
分為平日培養英語閱讀和寫作能力的方法，以及針對閱讀和寫作能力測驗的準備要點。

閱讀和寫作能力的模擬試題：
提供仿真模擬試題三回，並附上中文詳盡翻譯與解析。

企業英檢的必背520字：
提供出現頻率最高的520個單字，加上同義詞，皆為日常生活常用的字彙，宜勤加背誦。